SECURITY REVIVED

A.K. EVANS

Copyright 2019 by A.K. Evans
All rights reserved.

ISBN: 978-1-951441-07-4

No part of this book may be reproduced, distributer, or transmitted in any form or by any means including photocopying, recording, or other electronic or mechanical methods, without the prior written permission of the author except in the case of brief quotations in a book review.

This is a work of fiction. Names, characters, places, and incidents are the product of the author's imagination or are used fictitiously. Any resemblance to actual events, locales, or persons, living or dead, is coincidental.

Cover Artist
cover artwork © Sarah Hansen, Okay Creations
www.okaycreations.com

Editing & Proofreading
Ellie McLove, My Brother's Editor
www.mybrotherseditor.net

Formatting
Stacey Blake at Champagne Book Design
www.champagnebookdesign.com

REVIVED

PROLOGUE

Gunner

THE CROWD CHEERED WHEN THE SCORES WERE POSTED.

My name was in the number one spot.

Gunner Hayes.

As a twelve-year-old kid, I never thought I'd ever experience coming in first place in a snowboarding contest. Especially not when there were kids a few years older than me with far more experience competing against me.

But I'd done it.

About a month before my ninth birthday, I'd gone to a birthday party for a friend. His parents had paid for a group of friends to join him on the mountain for a day of snowboarding and skiing. I'd never done either.

My mom was a single mother who worked hard every day just to put food on the table, clothes on my back, and a roof over our head. So, I never had the opportunity to do something extravagant like trying out a winter sport like that. When I was invited to the all-expenses-paid party, I begged her to let me go.

I realized I wouldn't be able to show up empty-handed to the party, but we didn't really have the money for extras. I told her that I was willing to give up choosing a birthday present for myself just so I could get one for my friend and go to the party. It took a lot of begging, but she eventually gave in.

After that party, I was hooked. I came home telling my mom all about how much fun I had, and how I knew that becoming a professional snowboarder was what I wanted to do with my life. I was already a good student, but I promised I'd work even harder in school. And even though I helped my mom out a lot at home, I promised I'd do extra chores.

Anything.

I was willing to do anything to be able to get lessons and gear.

Once she saw how determined I was, my mom went above and beyond the call of duty. She already had a full-time job working days at the nursing home, but she ended up applying for a job at a diner as a waitress.

My mom loved me. It was just the two of us, and I appreciated everything she did for me. So, I made a promise to myself that I'd do everything I could to help her out when I could as well as work really hard at snowboarding. I wanted to make her proud. I didn't want her to think she'd made extra sacrifices for nothing.

And today, I was finally able to prove that to her.

The moment my name was posted on the board, I looked over at her. Tears were in her eyes, and there was a huge smile on her face. I made my way over to where she was standing and immediately wrapped my arms around her waist.

"I'm so proud of you, bub," she said as she hugged me back.

I squeezed her tight and replied, "Thanks, Mom."

"They're calling you up. Go get your medal," she urged me.

I pulled back, looked up at her, and saw nothing but pride in her eyes. Then I walked away to get my medal.

Two weeks later

"Please. Isn't there anything you can do?" my mom's worried voice said into the phone.

She didn't know I could hear her. I was supposed to be in my room studying for school but had walked out to use the bathroom. That's when I heard her on the phone.

I stood in the hallway of our apartment, hidden behind the wall, and listened to her pace the kitchen on the phone. I knew something was wrong.

"What about part-time?" she asked.

There was silence while she waited for whoever was on the phone to answer her question.

"Nothing?" she worried.

After another pause, she finally said, "Okay. Well, I'll stop in to pick up my final paycheck next week. And if anything at all changes, please call me immediately. I can come back."

I peeked around the corner and saw her hang up the phone before she lifted it from the cradle again and called someone.

"Hi, Denise. It's Cat. I was just wondering if there was any way I'd be able to pick up some extra shifts at the diner?"

Mom waited for Denise to answer her.

"Only one?" she asked.

Silence again.

She sighed before she spoke again. "I just got a call from human resources at the nursing home. Budget cuts are taking effect, and they've got to reduce their costs. I didn't make the first round of cuts, so I don't have that income anymore.

I was just barely making ends meet before, but we won't survive this on just my part-time hours at the diner."

She paused again before she insisted, "I know. I wouldn't want to take anyone else's hours away from them. But if there's anyone who needs coverage, I'll take it. No questions asked. I'm going to have to figure out where I can cut back in the meantime."

After a moment of silence, my mom asserted, "No. I know that's the obvious thing, but he's good. He's so good, Denise. He works really, really hard at snowboarding and just won his first contest a couple weeks ago. It's why I picked up the waitressing job to begin with. I wanted to give him this opportunity. But the sport is so expensive. Between the boards, boots, and the clothing he needs, it adds up so quickly. It's just that I know if we can tough it out for a little while, he's going to make it. Things will turn around."

Silence.

"Okay. Thank you. Like I said, whatever opens up, I'll take. I'll see you tomorrow morning then. Bye," she said.

I turned around and, as quietly as I could, went back down the hall to my room. I got back in my bed where my school books were, but I couldn't focus on my studying. My mom lost her job. And from what it sounded like, she wasn't going to be able to pay for the basic things we needed.

I needed to figure out a way to help my mom.

Sadly, by the time she came in my room to turn out my light and say goodnight, I hadn't figured anything out.

And with the weeks that followed, I saw just how much this had started to affect her. She was making so many sacrifices, and I don't think she realized that I noticed. But I did. When we had dinner together, I saw her put less and less food on her plate each time. Her dresses were bigger on her than they used to be. She also hadn't gotten her hair done in weeks.

The worst was the crying, though.

Every night after she'd come into my room and say goodnight, she'd go to her room and cry. I'm sure she had no idea that I could hear her. After listening to my mom cry herself to sleep night after night, I made a decision.

I had to quit snowboarding.

It was an expense we couldn't afford, and even if I could find a way to earn some money by shoveling snow or delivering newspapers, the money would be better spent on things we needed. My mom needed to eat more. She always looked tired and pale. And she was all I had in this world. Snowboarding would mean nothing to me if she wasn't around to see it.

So, the next day, I quit.

And I promised myself from that day forward that if I ever had the opportunity to have a family of my own, I'd never abandon them the way my father abandoned my mom and me.

CHAPTER 1

Gunner
Twenty-three years later

I WALKED THROUGH THE FRONT DOOR OF MY CONDO AND TOSSED my keys down on the table just inside the door without even looking to see where they landed. I'd done it hundreds of times before then. After hearing them clatter to the table, I moved to my bedroom and into the master bathroom where I turned on the shower.

It was late Friday night, and I'd just gotten home from a birthday party for my co-worker, Tyson. His girlfriend, Quinn, got together with his two sisters, his sister-in-law, and her sister to plan a party. Then they invited everybody to attend.

Tyson was not just a co-worker. He was one of my closest friends. In fact, most of the guys I worked with were men I'd consider to be more than just friendly acquaintances. Working for a private investigation firm required a level of trust with co-workers that I had a feeling was hard to find in a lot of careers.

So, when any one of them had something special happening in their lives, I had no problem joining them to celebrate.

And with the way things had been going lately, it seemed more and more of that would be happening as time went on.

Because somehow, even though all of us were single just a few years ago, all the guys I worked with at Cunningham Security had found someone special with whom to spend their life.

That is, all of them but me.

I was happy for my friends. Over the years, it had been something else to see them all fall for the love of a good woman. Now, some of them were married, some already had kids, some had babies on the way, some were engaged, and others were just enjoying the company of the woman in their life.

It was great to see that they'd all found happiness, the kind that I had no doubt would last a lifetime.

But as I looked around the room at Tyson's party for the few hours I was there, all of my friends there with their significant others, I found myself longing for that for myself. I'd always wanted that. Ever since I was little, I knew I wanted that.

A family.

Sure, I'd had my mom.

And she loved me enough for both her and my non-existent father. But I knew I wanted more in life. I wanted a lifelong companion. Someone with whom I could share my life, grow old, and have my own children.

As I stood under the hot spray of the shower, I considered my current situation.

Perhaps coming home after Tyson's party wasn't the best way to try and get myself out there to find a woman, but I knew where me going out to a bar tonight would lead. I'd end up having a one-night stand with a random woman I hadn't ever seen before. It'd be great for the time being, but then it'd be over. I should know. I'd had them before. There was nothing necessarily wrong with having a one-night stand; I passed no judgment on anyone who had them. But it wasn't what I wanted anymore.

Finishing up in the shower, I turned off the water and stepped out to towel off. After I was done in the bathroom, I hung up the towel and walked back out to my bedroom. I slid into my bed and rested my head back on the pillow. It was then, as I stared up at the ceiling, that I decided I'd have to start making an effort during the daytime to get myself out to more locations where I'd be able to find the kind of woman I wanted. If going out every night or every weekend wasn't how I wanted to spend the rest of my life, I didn't think it made much sense to go searching for a woman in a bar at that hour.

Letting out a deep sigh, I reached out to my nightstand for my remote and flipped on the television. The moment the picture was on the screen, I gasped. It took me a second to realize what I was seeing. I sat up in my bed and stared. If I had thought my mind was playing tricks on me, the name along the bottom of the screen would have confirmed that wasn't the case.

Because there she was.

The girl I had spent nearly all of my teenage years having wet dreams about.

Sage Thompson.

She was reporting on the weather, and she was as stunning as ever. My heart was pounding hard and fast in my chest as I listened to her talk. Apparently, there were threats of several hurricanes along the east coast in the coming days, but I really couldn't pay attention to anything concerning the weather.

Because I was completely caught up in seeing her for the first time in nearly twenty years. Knowing a lot could have happened in that time, my eyes went to her left hand. It was bare. The feeling that swept through me when I saw that is something I couldn't even begin to describe. Relief might have been the best word for it. Relief that perhaps she was single and I'd have the chance that I should have taken years ago.

I couldn't get over how beautiful she was. The girl I'd known in high school was all grown up. She was wearing a form-fitting dress that stopped an inch or so above her knees. It was easy to see the gorgeous curves she'd developed over the years.

I struggled and failed not to make a sound, thinking about how badly I wanted to feel her body against mine… under it, too.

Fuck.

Sage was making me feel like a teenage boy all over again, and she was doing it right through the television screen.

Making a split-second decision, I flung the covers off my body and got myself dressed. Then, I was out the door, in my truck, and on my way to the local news station.

I hadn't been parked there more than ten minutes when I saw the door open.

Sage was walking out.

Knowing what I wanted, I decided my best option was to just walk right up to her. If I spent too much time thinking about it, it was likely I'd end up just turning around and heading home. I wasn't going to make that mistake again. So, I opened my door and walked in Sage's direction.

She was walking in the parking lot with her head down, her attention on her phone in her hand. Once I was close enough to her, I called, "Sage."

Sage was startled. She immediately stopped her strides and looked up. Her eyes connected with mine and narrowed briefly before they widened and she replied, "Gunner?"

Fuck.

Fuck.

She remembered me.

The sound of my name coming from her lips was too much to handle. All of it was.

Seeing her there, knowing she recognized me, remembered me, and looked as beautiful as she did, I wondered if it was possible to fall in love on the spot. Maybe this feeling I felt in my chest was love at first sight… even though I'd met her so long ago.

Never had I ever felt anything like it before now. It started the minute I saw her on my television screen, and it only grew the moment I saw her standing in front of me. With each second that passed, it grew stronger and stronger.

Realizing I probably looked like an idiot standing there without saying anything to her, I nodded and confirmed she'd guessed right.

Sage stared at me, shock moving through her features, before she suddenly shook it off and launched herself into my arms. "Oh my God!" she cried. "It's so good to see you. How are you?"

I took the force of her body weight as she threw herself into my arms. Holding her body tight against mine, I couldn't remember anything in my life feeling better than that.

"I saw you on television tonight," I started. "After nearly twenty years, I had to come down here to see you in person."

Sage pulled her arms from around my neck and slid her hands down until her palms were pressed against my chest. She looked up at me with her big, beautiful eyes and sighed, "I'm so glad that you did. Wow, it's so great seeing you again."

I couldn't help but smile at her.

For some reason, I couldn't get over just how breathtaking she was. Even though I'd known her since high school and had seen her giving the weather report, seeing her now was like looking at her for the first time.

And it was like I'd gone from feeling like the lone wolf at Tyson's party to suddenly having a fire lit inside me. Maybe Sage was my chance at finding the same happiness that all of my friends had already found. It was like I'd gone from feeling numb inside to being revived. And when I thought about that, I realized that only someone like Sage could do that.

"It's great to see you, too," I returned. "Do you have plans now? Or can I convince you to join me for a cup of coffee so we can catch up?"

"Coffee?" she asked. "At this hour?"

It was approaching eleven o'clock, but I didn't care. I didn't think I'd be able to walk away from her tonight.

"They have decaf," I noted with a grin.

Sage let out a laugh. "I guess you're right. Okay. Let's go get a cup of coffee and catch up."

"Really?" I asked. I hadn't meant to sound so shocked, but I was. I guess I never thought she would have agreed. But apparently, I was no longer afraid of rejection. A man without anything doesn't have anything to lose.

Sage nodded. "Yeah. But I've only been back in town for a few weeks now. You're going to have to tell me where the best place to go is."

"We can go to Colvert's," I declared. "It's right around the corner from where I work, and it's not too far from here. Have you heard of it?"

She shook her head.

"Okay. Do you want to ride with me then?" I asked.

Sage thought for a moment but ultimately shook her head. "I probably shouldn't leave my car here. My co-workers might see it here in the parking lot and get concerned.

To say I was disappointed was an understatement, but I completely understood her predicament. I just didn't want to let her out of my sight now.

"Where is your car?" I wondered, looking around the lot.

She pointed to the SUV parked right beside my truck. I smiled and walked beside her to it. When we made it to her door and she pushed the button to unlock the car, I opened her door and saw the smile spread across her face.

After she got in, I informed her, "I'm in the truck right next to you. Just follow me."

"Okay." She beamed, the light in her face nearly blinding me.

With that, I closed her door and quickly hopped in my truck.

As I drove to Colvert's, I glanced up in my rearview mirror several times. Part of me was still in shock that I was seeing her for the first time in all these years. It felt like I was getting a second chance.

I met Sage back when we were both sophomores in high school. The very first time I laid my eyes on her, I was certain I had fallen in love. All those years ago, she was beautiful. And I found it extremely intimidating.

Sage was always such a sweetheart, too. So, I had no idea why I never asked her out. Even if she didn't want to go out with me, I didn't think she had a mean bone in her body. She would have been nice about it.

But for some reason, I couldn't. Maybe it was that I just didn't think she'd ever say yes. And the fear of rejection was too much. Anyone else, I wouldn't have cared. Sage was someone special, though. Perhaps I thought that if I didn't ask, there was always hope that it could happen one day in the future. If I risked it then and she rejected me, though, I didn't think I would have ever recovered from that.

Two months before our junior year ended, Sage left. Her father was transferred to a different location for work, so she had to leave. And I never forgot the day she left. It was the first time in my life that I ever truly felt regret.

We pulled into the lot behind Colvert's and parked. I got out and met Sage at her door. Then the two of us walked together to the front door. I kept my hand pressed to the small of her back, guiding her the whole way there.

After we were inside and had both ordered a cup of coffee, Sage simply stared across the table at me and grinned.

"What?" I asked.

She shook her head slightly and answered, "Nothing. I'm sorry. You must think I'm a total goof. It's just that I'm in such shock right now. When I woke up this morning, I never expected I'd walk out of work tonight to see you."

Letting out a chuckle, I agreed, "I feel the same way. I was just at a birthday party for my co-worker. I got home, showered, got in bed, and turned on the television. There you were."

"There I was," she whispered.

I dipped my chin and gave her a nod.

"So, you know where I work," she started. "And you said this place is close to your job. Where do you work? What are you doing with yourself these days?"

"I actually work right around the corner at Cunningham Security. It's a private investigation and security firm," I replied.

Sage looked genuinely surprised by this news. "Wow. Really? When you say security, do you mean like home security or personal security?"

"Both. We don't need to provide personal security for individuals very often, but it happens every now and then. In fact, a couple years ago, my boss' wife who happened to just be his girlfriend at the time had a stalker. She had round-the-clock coverage until we were able to figure out who her stalker was," I explained.

"That's crazy. Is it dangerous?" she wondered.

I shrugged. "The average person might think so. But it's usually pretty routine stuff we're dealing with. It's not very often we have cases that are extremely dangerous. But it does happen. We're trained, so it doesn't ever feel bad in the moment."

Sage gave me a nod of understanding.

"What about you?" I asked. "You said you've been back in town only for a few weeks. Is this the first you've been back since you left all those years ago?"

"Yeah," she answered. "After my parents told me we were moving to Oregon back then, I remember being so devastated. I was actually really angry at them for uprooting our lives right at the end of my high school years."

I hated that for her. It never really dawned on me at the time, but now that I thought about it, I guess it couldn't have been easy for her to move several states away and start all over again. If she'd been in elementary school, maybe it would have been easier. But as a high school student entering her senior year, I couldn't imagine it was any fun.

"Was it rough for you?" I asked.

"At first," she admitted. "Initially, when I got there, I was really closed off. I hated being in a new town with new people. I just wanted to come back home. So, the remainder of my junior year was pretty terrible. It's not that anybody was mean to me or anything. I just didn't really make the effort to make any friends. But over the summer, I decided to make the most of my situation. I explored my new hometown, met some friends, and ended up having a great senior year."

Hearing that made me feel better.

"Did you stay out there for college then?" I questioned her.

Nodding, Sage replied, "Yes. I had considered coming back here, but I thought about the fact that everyone I was friends with here would also be going off to college. It wasn't likely that all those familiar faces would be sticking around here anyway. Where did you go?"

"Believe it or not, I went into the Army. When I got out, I came back here and haven't left since."

"There's just something about this place that feels like home, am I right?" she asked.

Holding her gaze, I agreed, "Yeah. Is that why you came back?"

Sage nodded.

It's like I'm getting a second chance, I thought.

"What?" Sage broke into my thoughts.

"What what?"

"You said something about a second chance," she shared.

Fuck.

I said that aloud.

With nothing to lose, I decided to just go for it. "I'll never forget your last day at school here in Windsor. All I can remember from that day was how much I hated myself and how much of a fool I was."

Sage's brows pulled together. "What do you mean? Why?"

"Because ever since I first met you in tenth grade, I had a crush on you," I confessed. "But I never had the courage to ask you out. When you left, I was so upset because I didn't think I was ever going to get the chance again."

Shock registered on her face.

"Really?"

I nodded.

Sage bit her lip, and I could see her mind working. She was struggling with something, but eventually blurted, "Every day for two years, I hoped you would ask me out. I thought you were the cutest boy in school, and I wanted to be your girlfriend so bad."

Fuck.

Fuck.

"Are you serious?" I asked.

Sage dipped her chin.

"You mean, all these years we could have been together?"

She shrugged. "I don't know how a long-distance thing would have worked out, but I would have loved having the chance to try."

I had to go for it. She hadn't mentioned a boyfriend, so I was going to go for it. "Are you seeing anyone now?" I wondered.

Sage shook her head.

"Do you want to be?" I pressed.

"Are you asking for yourself?" she retorted.

I simply grinned at her.

She smiled back at me.

"Do you want to get out of here?"

"Yeah," she whispered her response.

With that, I threw some money down on the table, took Sage's hand in mine, and left. Then, since it was closer, Sage followed me back to my place.

CHAPTER 2

Sage

I DIDN'T KNOW HOW THIS HAPPENED.

I didn't know how it was possible that the boy I'd had a crush on through most of my high school years had admitted me to me nearly twenty years too late that he felt the same about me.

But even if I thought too much time had passed, it was apparent Gunner knew just how to make up for lost time.

Because I was currently in his bed, completely naked, and his mouth was between my legs. I was on the verge of another orgasm.

When we got back to his place a little while ago, we didn't waste any more time. We barely got ourselves inside the door when Gunner tugged me toward him and pressed his lips to mine. That first kiss was everything I imagined it would have been and more.

And from that point forward, it had been all about exploring each other and realizing precisely what we'd missed out on all these years. Gunner was an incredible lover. Not only was his body perfect from head to toe, but he knew exactly how to use it, too.

We'd stripped each other out of our clothes, and I was

surprised at how willing we both seemed to be about not rushing it.

The memory of Gunner unzipping my dress and slowly removing it from my body flitted through my brain, and I knew it was something I'd never forget. Then, the way he looked at me when I stood in front of him wearing nothing but a lacy bra and a lace-trimmed thong was forever engrained in my mind.

"Take off your bra," he requested.

I did.

When it fell to the floor, I watched as his chest began to rise and fall. Seeing that indicated to me that he felt just as many emotions as I did at that moment.

"Panties," he rasped next.

I hooked my thumbs into the material at my hips and pushed them down my legs. His eyes roamed over my body, clearly appreciating everything he saw.

"You're so beautiful, Sage," he said, his voice husky.

"Don't leave me out here alone," I begged, seeing him there bare-chested with his pants still on.

Luckily, he understood what I wanted and wasted no time in removing the rest of his clothes. And that's when I got further proof that Gunner really liked what he saw when he looked at me.

I took two steps toward him and stopped because he had already started moving my way. And when he was less than an arm's length away from me, he reached out and tugged me toward him. Our bodies collided as he captured my mouth with his.

I loved feeling the warmth of his body against mine. But even more than that, I loved how he continued to kiss me while he allowed his fingertips to roam over my skin.

When he'd done enough exploring with his hands, Gunner lifted me up with an arm at my waist and one at my thigh. I had no choice but to wrap my legs around him. The moment I did, he began moving.

Up until this point, I'd loved everything Gunner had done. But what he did next made my heart soar. It started with the way he lowered me to my back in his bed. He'd done it so slow and gentle, like he was handling the most delicate piece of porcelain.

Gunner pulled his mouth from mine and slid his lips down along the skin of my throat. On the way, he'd occasionally stop and use his tongue to taste me. Then he'd keep going. And the entire time I felt the whisper-soft touches of his mouth on my skin, his hands were on my breasts, teasing me.

I opened my eyes when I no longer felt Gunner's mouth on my body, only to find him staring down at me with such intensity and adoration.

"Sage," he whispered, closing his eyes. When he opened them again, he continued, "Look at you. So beautiful, naked in my bed. What did I do to deserve this?"

He was killing me. Not only was he continuing to say such wonderful things to me, but he was also running his thumbs over my nipples. I was so turned on, I couldn't stop myself from moaning. Gunner was on his knees, one of them between my legs. So, when I moaned, I instinctively rubbed the most intimate part of my body against his thigh.

Gunner felt it and heard it. From what I could tell, he loved it.

Because the growl that tore out of him was like nothing I'd ever heard before. No sooner did he emit that sound when he dropped down to suck one of my nipples into his mouth. While he concentrated a good amount of his effort on what his mouth was doing to my breast, his hand wasn't slacking either. It had left the opposite breast and began drifting down my abdomen until he reached the prize.

And while I was sure he viewed it as a prize, I had no doubts that I was the one who was currently winning. Gunner slid one finger through my wetness, causing me to arch my back off the bed and press my breast further into his mouth. Doing that only served to make him give me even more. He pressed his fingertips flat against my vagina and circled them, giving me the friction I had been so desperately seeking only moments before against his thigh.

"Gunner," I breathed.

The second his name left my lips, he slid one finger inside me.

"Baby," I moaned.

Gunner slipped a second finger inside. Then he gave me what I needed. He worked his fingers, pumping them in and out of me, as his mouth stayed devoted to my breast. He licked and sucked, never once relenting.

It took me almost no time at all to get to that point where I was on the verge of an orgasm. I was moving my hips, riding his fingers, clenching my hands into fists, and moaning with such pleasure.

"Kiss me," I begged, feeling myself so close.

Gunner did precisely as I asked. And when he did, I came apart. My body shuddered with the pleasure he'd given me. He slowed the strokes of his fingers as he saw me through to the end.

My body completely relaxed, and he pulled back just a touch to smile against my lips. "You're so sexy," he whispered.

"Mmm," I responded.

Gunner let out a chuckle before he slid his fingers from

my body and leaned over to his nightstand. Seconds later, he had rolled on a condom.

When he settled himself between my thighs, he asked, "Do you have any stamina left?"

My eyes, which had been closed, fluttered open at the feel of the tip of him at my entrance. After the orgasm he'd delivered, I could have easily drifted off to sleep. But feeling him right there, I was suddenly wide awake and completely revived again.

"I can muster up a bit," I assured him.

When Gunner made no move to push inside, I began to squirm. When he still made no move, I offered some encouragement. "Take me, Gunner. I want to feel you inside me."

That was all the encouragement he needed. Because the next thing I knew, he was sliding inside.

And he felt spectacular.

Perfect.

Made for me.

"Fuck," he muttered when he'd buried himself to the root. "Sage, you're perfect. You feel so beautiful."

God, I loved that.

I loved hearing him say that.

My emotions were getting the best of me, but I still managed to croak, "So do you."

Gunner's eyes were searching my face. I didn't know what he was looking for or if he found it. All I knew was I couldn't take much more of this without him moving inside me.

"Make love to me, Gunner," I pleaded with him.

His features softened only seconds before he began moving. And when he did, he did it slow and sweet. He wasn't even remotely interested in rushing things. Knowing he wanted to take his time with me had my heart skipping a beat.

When Gunner and I sat across from each other in the café earlier and admitted our feelings to one another I knew what I wanted with him… what we both wanted with one another. And from the moment I got in my car to follow Gunner back to his place, I imagined what it would be like.

To my surprise, what I imagined wasn't anything like what it had turned out to be. Because I found the reality was far better than anything I could have dreamt up in my mind.

We took our time, our bodies moving together in perfect synchronicity. At first, I was on my back. But eventually, Gunner rolled so he was on his back. And when I finally came apart on top of him, Gunner watched. It was only then that he allowed himself to have the same.

My body collapsed on his, and Gunner allowed me to stay planted on his chest for a while. After some time had passed, though, he gently rolled me to the side and said, "I'll be right back."

When he returned, he slid in next to me and curled my body into his. For a long time, he didn't say anything. He simply held me close and traced his fingers lightly over the skin at my hip.

Until only a few moments ago.

When he apparently had had enough of a break and wanted more.

Or, at least, wanted to give me more.

Because his mouth was between my legs. And his tongue was doing things that I didn't even know were possible. He'd been licking, sucking, flicking, circling, and tasting for what felt like an endless amount of time. He was so good at it, too.

I reached my hand down and clutched his hair in my grasp.

"I'm going to come," I warned him.

I lost his mouth momentarily, but it was only long enough for him to order, "Give it to me."

So, that's what I did.

And seconds after he'd taken that from me, he rolled on another condom and gave me something in return.

Gunner left me in his bed again while he went to dispose of the condom after we finished a second round. When he returned, I started to roll toward the opposite edge of the bed. I sat up and declared, "I should probably get going."

Before I had the chance to get up and get my clothes, Gunner hooked an arm around my waist and pulled me back toward him.

"Stay," he urged. "I'm not done with you yet."

"But—"

Gunner cut me off. "Stay," he repeated, his tone much firmer.

It dawned on me that he said he wasn't done with me yet. "How can you possibly have the energy for another round?" I asked.

With his front pressed to my back and his arm draped over the side of my body, Gunner explained, "We're going to rest for a little bit first. Then we'll go for another round or two."

"Another round or two?" I repeated.

Gunner didn't reply. He simply gave me a squeeze and touched his lips to my shoulder, kissing me softly.

And it wasn't long before I allowed my sated body to give in to sleep.

I wasn't sure what time it was when it happened, but I knew I had just barely recovered when Gunner woke me up sometime in the middle of the night for round three. He woke me up and was relentlessly teasing me. It didn't take long for me to lose my patience and push him to his back so I could climb on and get what I needed.

Then we both fell back asleep.

And when I woke up on my own a few hours after that, I slunk out of Gunner's place without waking him.

Gunner

I didn't even have to open my eyes to know she wasn't in bed with me. Even still, I opened them and confirmed what I already knew was the case.

Sage wasn't there.

While part of me was hoping she'd gotten up to use the bathroom or get herself a cup of coffee, my instincts told me that I'd get up and prove that I wasn't that lucky. I had no doubts about it.

Sage left.

And I couldn't understand why she would do that without waking me first.

Last night meant everything to me. I knew that we hadn't even been reconnected with one another for a full twenty-four hours at this point, but that didn't matter. What I felt with her was real, and it was more than anything I'd ever felt before with anyone else in my life.

She felt it. There was no way she didn't feel even a fraction of what I did last night.

But the nagging worry still lingered in the back of my mind. Because knowing how I felt about our night together, I couldn't understand why Sage would walk away from me at some point early this morning without saying anything to me.

I hoped she wasn't plagued with regret. That would have been the absolute worst outcome that I could imagine from this. Something that made me feel so alive could have possibly made her feel disappointment… either with herself or with me.

How could she have felt regret about what we had last night? It was too good. It felt like it had been a long time coming. It felt like it was something that should have happened years earlier.

Nothing else made sense, though.

And I realized that if I didn't get up and reach out to Sage, I'd spend the rest of my morning running through a million dreadful scenarios about it. I figured it was best to just reach out to her and figure out the best way to quell any fears or worries she had about what happened between us.

Sadly, I hadn't managed to get Sage's number before things got heated last night. But that wouldn't be a problem. Being a private investigator had its perks, so I had easy ways of getting something as simple as a phone number. Luckily, I had access to what I needed to find her number without needing to head into the office.

I got out of bed, pulled on a pair of pants, and moved to my office. Opening my laptop and the program I needed to find what I was looking for, I got to work. It didn't take long before I found Sage's number and punched it into my cell.

It rang several times before I was greeted by her voicemail. *"Hey, it's Sage. Sorry I missed your call. Leave me a message, and I'll get back to you as soon as I can."*

Her voice.

I already missed the sound of her voice.

"Sage, it's Gunner. I didn't expect you'd be gone when I woke up this morning. Please give me a call so we can talk."

I disconnected the call, closed my laptop, and sat there staring off into space. This was not even close to what I had imagined. As I sat there, I had a million thoughts running through my mind. Regret and embarrassment were the only things that continued to plague me. Not that I felt those things. But I worried that Sage did. I had this awful, sneaking suspicion that she woke up at some point early this morning, realized we hadn't even gone on a proper date, and she'd given herself to me the way that she did. Multiple times. Either she was bothered by it after the fact, thinking that I'd be judging her for that, or perhaps she didn't enjoy it.

I didn't know which was worse.

But when I really thought about it, I didn't think it was a matter of not liking what she got from me. Unless she managed to convince herself in her mind that she didn't, I knew her body was a different story. She responded to my touch. Her moans and whimpers last night confirmed that her body wasn't the problem.

Which meant it was all in her heart and her head.

And I knew that was going to be a tough thing to break through if she was as strong-willed as I believed her to be.

Just as I took a deep breath in and sighed it out, my phone buzzed in my hand. I looked down, saw it was Sage, and felt my heart start pounding.

"Sage," I greeted her.

"Hey, Gunner," she said softly. Her voice was just a touch over a whisper.

"You left," I told her something she already knew.

"I know. I'm sorry for not waking you, but I had to go," she returned. "How did you get my number?"

Fuck. Was she pissed at me?

"I'm a private investigator," I answered.

"Oh, right. That makes sense. Listen, I can't really talk right now, but I wanted to at least return your call."

I didn't think it was wise for us to put off talking about what happened between us last night. I thought it was best to get it out in the open right away. So, I advised, "I don't think it's a good idea to wait. I think we should talk."

"I can't," she insisted.

She was about to say something else, but I cut in. "Sage, honey, whatever it is, we have to talk about it. I'd rather know now. Was it not good for you? Do you regret what we had last night?"

"Not at all," she whispered. "It was... Gunner, it was incredible."

Well, there was at least that.

Before I could respond, Sage's voice got even quieter, and she shared, "I can still feel you."

"What?"

"There," she started. "Between my legs. I can still feel you there. And I love it."

"So, why did you leave?" I asked.

There was a moment of hesitation before she explained, "Because I had to catch a flight. I'm leaving town—"

With the sinking feeling in the pit of my stomach, I cut her off. "Where are you going?"

"The east coast," she replied.

Fuck.

Fuck.

"Why?"

"It's for work. There are two storms that I've got to cover. I'll be in North Carolina."

The hurricanes she was reporting on last night. Fucking hurricanes. Most people fled areas where storms were going to be bad, but Sage was headed right for that danger. And it scared the living daylights out of me.

"Will you be safe?" I asked.

"It's like you said to me last night," she started. "To the average person, it might seem that way. But I know what I'm doing and how to track a storm. Obviously, there are factors and a storm can sometimes be unpredictable, but we do what we have to do to keep ourselves safe. I'll be okay."

I didn't know what had gotten into me, but I felt an overwhelming sense of dread come over me. "Promise me you'll come back home to me," I ordered, my voice thick with emotion.

Sage didn't immediately respond. After a long hesitation, she promised, "I'll come back home to you, Gunner."

Hearing those words allowed some of the tension to leave my body. It wasn't all gone, but I felt substantially better.

"I have to go now," Sage said. "They already told us to turn off our devices, and the flight attendant is giving me dirty looks."

"Okay, Sage. Stay safe, honey."

"I will."

With that, I disconnected my call with Sage. Then, I spent the rest of my day watching the weather reports regarding the impending hurricanes on the east coast.

CHAPTER 3

Sage

There were three quick knocks on the door of my hotel room.

Finally.

My food was here.

Even though the clock indicated it had only been thirty minutes since I'd ordered the room service, it felt like it had been much longer than that. Of course, I'd waited until the point I was beyond famished to order something to eat.

I hadn't done it on purpose, though. It was just that it had been a long day of traveling for me and two of my co-workers, Jack and Dennis. While I was the lucky one who'd stand in front of the camera while we covered the storms, they were the men behind the lens. Once Jack, Dennis, and I arrived in North Carolina, we had to drive from the airport to our hotel. The three of us dumped our bags off there and immediately headed out to scope out the area.

The coastal towns all along the North Carolina coastline were expected to receive the brunt of the storms. We wanted to capture some footage and still shots of the location before the storms hit because we had a feeling based on the models I'd been reviewing with my team back in Windsor that these towns were no longer going to look the way they currently did once the storms passed.

After we got our footage, Jack, Dennis, and I checked out the beaches. Even though the first of the two storms wasn't supposed to make landfall until late Monday morning, we could already see the beginnings of it in the ocean. The waves coming in weren't calm or slow as they crashed along the shore. I knew they were only going to increase in size and speed as the storm approached.

Following our time at the beach, we decided to head back to the hotel for the evening. The guys were sharing a room next to mine. Being the only woman in the group, I lucked out and got a room all to myself.

I was thankful for that for a multitude of reasons, the first of those being that I was able to strip down and get a shower right away. I felt completely gross from the plane ride and the mix of the salty air. But the most notable reason I was grateful was that now that my food had arrived, I could finally eat my food quickly and make the phone call I'd been thinking about making all day long.

So, without delaying myself any longer, I ran to the door, opened it, and signed for the room service delivery. I wheeled the cart over to the edge of my bed and sat down in front of it. After I pulled the silver cover off the top of the plate, I dumped some ketchup on my cheeseburger and devoured half of it in no time at all. I probably would have finished the entire thing in that time, but I was also shoveling fries in at the same time. When I managed to get the rest of my burger down, I wheeled the cart back outside the door and locked myself inside my room, where I planned to be for the remainder of the night.

No sooner did I flop down on the massive, king-size bed

when I began to regret my decision to eat so fast. The hunger pains had taken over, though, and made me ravenous.

As I laid there giving myself a minute to allow my food to digest, I had one thing on my mind. And it had nothing to do with the impending storms.

Nope.

All I was thinking about was one man.

Gunner Hayes.

As crazy as it sounded, even to myself, I missed him like crazy. I hadn't even been away from him for a full twenty-four hours yet, but I missed him like it had been years since I'd laid my eyes on him.

Was it not good for you? Do you regret what we had last night?

Those two questions haunted my brain throughout the entire flight. How it was possible that Gunner could think I didn't like what we'd shared was beyond me. And regret? The only regret I would have had would have been not seizing that opportunity to be with him last night. There wasn't one single thing about our night together that I regretted.

Not only did I have those two questions he asked running through my mind all day, but also the worry and desperation in his voice throughout most of our conversation. I had to admit that even though I didn't like knowing he was so upset and was thinking the worst about why I left without waking him, it felt so good to hear how much it mattered to him.

The truth was, until he showed up outside my news station last night, I had been wondering if perhaps I'd missed my shot at finding my happily ever after. I knew that being thirty-five didn't exactly make me old, but I had started to wonder what my single status made men who might have been interested in me think. I wondered if they had assumed I was still single because I was crazy or something.

Of course, there was nothing wrong with being single. For the most part, I was happy. I liked my job, had a good relationship with my parents, and kept in touch with my friends from Oregon. I led a fulfilled life. But I still had been longing for something more. And because I hadn't found it, I'd noticed how much it was playing on my mind. It was a big part of the reason why I moved back to Wyoming. I needed a change, and I didn't truly feel like I was home until I was back in Windsor.

Seeing Gunner waiting for me when I walked out of work last night solidified for me that I'd made the right choice. What happened from the moment I threw myself into his arms in that parking lot until I disconnected my call with him this morning dispelled any of the fears I had about something being wrong with me. Beyond that, I had initially wondered after I left his place this morning how he'd react to our blissful night of passion. After that call with him, I no longer had any concerns about that either.

And considering he'd done such a wonderful job of reassuring me about how he felt about everything between us, I wanted to do something similar for him. So, I reached out and grabbed my cell phone off the nightstand. Going to my recent calls, I found Gunner's name, which I'd immediately programmed into my cell after our call earlier, at the top of that list.

After two rings, he answered, "Sage? Are you okay?"

I smiled, loving how it felt to have his concern. "I'm learning a hard lesson right now," I replied.

"What does that mean?" he asked, sounding a bit alarmed.

"Well, when my cameramen, Jack and Dennis, and I arrived here earlier today, we got to work right away. As a result, we spent most of the day out and about, checking out the area and capturing footage and still shots for our reports. But we hadn't stopped to eat anything. Now, I'm laying here in my bed in this hotel, and I can't even move because I stuffed myself so full with room service."

Gunner let out a laugh. "You ate too much?" he confirmed.

"Technically speaking, I'm probably still under the recommended calorie count today since that was really all I ate, but it was definitely too much food for one sitting. I barely stopped to breathe."

"Don't do that again," he warned me.

"What? Eat fast?" I asked.

"Well, yeah. That and not eat all day. That's not good for you," he informed me.

I couldn't really make him any guarantees considering I didn't know what was ahead for the next few days, but I also wanted him to know that it wasn't the norm for me to skip meals either. "I was running behind today," I started. "I would have had breakfast, but by the time I woke up, I realized I was going to miss my flight if I didn't hurry. I just didn't have time."

"You should have said something to me last night," he advised. "I would have made sure you were up on time."

I burst out laughing.

"What's so funny?" he wondered when my laughing had subsided.

"When would I have told you last night? We were occupied with so much other stuff," I noted.

There was a bit of a pause before he said softly, "Yeah, I guess we were."

"I really had a great time with you, Gunner," I shared, believing he deserved to know the truth. I knew this was something we would have discussed this morning had I not left before we had the chance. So, I thought it would be nice of me to give him this for now. I continued, "More than that, I'm happy I came home to Windsor and that it was you who came to meet me outside the news station last night."

"Me too, Sage," he agreed. "I just hope that second storm weakens between now and the time it's supposed to make landfall."

"Have you been watching the weather reports?" I asked.

"All fucking day," he admitted, sounding utterly defeated. "I'm so worried about you."

He was making me fall harder and harder for him with every word he spoke to me. I knew how good Gunner could make my body feel; he'd already irrevocably proved that to me. But the fact that he said all the right things and had no problems communicating exactly how he felt was a big deal to me. I loved that he had such a genuine level of concern for my safety and didn't mind sharing it either.

"Okay, listen to me," I ordered. "I expect I'll be spending the better part of the day tomorrow reporting on the first storm. It sounds like you already know that it's going to be a bad one, but the second storm is the one we're really concerned about. The first one is expected to make landfall early Monday morning. When the worst of either storm hits, I might not be able to be reached. We'll just have to see how it goes. We'll take shelter in our hotel when it's hitting us the worst. After it passes, I'll be back out there reporting on it. People will want to know what the extent of the damage is, and they'll need to know how to best prepare for the second one that's expected to arrive a few days later. But no matter what, Gunner, I'm going to try to touch base with you every day. I am going to promise you right now that I will do what I can to let you know that I'm okay. I can't make promises about what time of day you'll hear from me, but I promise to try to do it every day."

Gunner didn't respond. He was quiet for so long that I began to grow concerned.

"Gunner?" I called.

"Yeah?" he replied, his voice a deep rasp.

"Are you okay?"

I heard him take in a deep breath. "I'm so scared for you, Sage. I like being in control of situations, and I can't control this situation."

"I'm a smart woman, Gunner. I'm good at my job, and I can assess the situation before doing something that's too risky. You need to have faith in me that I know what I'm doing," I urged him.

"Sage, honey, this isn't about making you feel like you aren't a capable woman. I have zero doubts about that. But things changed for me last night. You told me you weren't seeing anyone. And not long after I asked you if you wanted to be, your gorgeous, naked body was in my bed. You're my woman now, and I don't want you in any danger. Ever."

I sat there in silence wondering if it was too soon. Could I fall in love with a man in less than a day? Or was I being stupid?

I never came up with an answer, but I knew I liked Gunner referring to me as his woman.

"You're not saying anything," he noted after some time had passed without a response from me.

"This is fast," I rasped, feeling compelled to be honest with him.

"I had a crush on you when I was fifteen years old," he declared. "According to what you said last night, you had one on me, too. We're thirty-five now. You're talking about twenty years now. That's not fast. In fact, it feels like I've been waiting for you forever."

I loved that he felt that way because if I was being honest, I felt similarly. But I didn't want us to be blinded by the newness and the excitement of what we'd started. Surely, we could both end up being very hurt in the process if we weren't careful. At that thought, I felt my body shudder. Now that I had Gunner back in my life after all these years, I didn't want to think about losing him again. Years ago, I had no choice. My parents were moving. But now, I had a say in the matter.

"I love that you care enough to be this worried about me," I finally said.

"Do you know when you'll be back?" he asked.

"I'm scheduled to fly back two weeks from today," I responded. "Obviously, that all depends on how these storms pan out. If it gets really bad out there, things could change. I don't know for sure what'll happen, but I should have a better idea as we get closer to that time."

Gunner let out a groan of displeasure. "I'm going to be glued to the television for the next two weeks," he shared.

"I'm sorry," I lamented.

"Don't be. At least I'll be able to see you," he pointed out.

The second he said those words, I realized how unfair it was and didn't hesitate to let him know it either. "That's not right," I announced.

"What isn't?" he wondered.

"You get to see me, but I don't get to see you," I clarified.

After a brief pause, my phone began ringing. Pulling my phone away from my ear, I realized that Gunner was starting a video chat with me. I didn't waste any time answering it. The next thing I knew, Gunner's handsome face was on my screen smiling back at me.

"That's so much better," I claimed. "You've just made my night."

I watched as Gunner's features softened. "I'm happy I could do that for you, Sage."

"Well considering it's going to be two weeks before you can do anything else for me…" I trailed off, hoping he understood the meaning in my statement.

He cocked an eyebrow. "Is that a challenge, Miss Thompson?"

"It wasn't intended to be, but the fact that you think it was certainly has me intrigued now," I remarked.

"Show me what you're wearing," he ordered.

I sat up a little straighter. "What?" I asked.

"Show me," he repeated in an encouraging tone.

I angled the phone out in front of me to show him what I was wearing. A pair of panties and a camisole. When I pointed the camera back to my face, I noticed the look in his had changed.

"What's wrong?" I pressed him.

"I thought twenty years was a long time," he started. "These two weeks are going to feel like an eternity."

I couldn't stop a laugh from escaping. "That's because you've had me now, handsome. You know what I feel like. You know how I taste. And you know what I look like when you make me come."

"I'm supposed to be making you feel good right now," he rumbled. "What are you trying to do to me, Sage?"

"Giving you the same," I explained. "I don't want to do this alone."

He shook his head. "No, babe. This is for you this time."

He thought he was going to resist me? He thought he deserved to see me come, but I didn't warrant the same?

Gunner had another thing coming if that's how he thought this was going to go.

A devious grin formed on my face. "Tell me, handsome," I started. "How do I taste?"

Gunner's eyes remained focused on me, and they were growing intense. He stayed silent.

I tipped my head to one side and gave him a pouty face. "Didn't I taste good?" I wondered.

"The best I've ever had the pleasure of tasting," he assured me.

I pulled the phone away from my body a bit so he could still see my face, but also my breasts. They were still covered by my white camisole as I brought my hand up, cupped one breast, and stroked my thumb over my nipple. It was hard within seconds, and I knew he could see it through the material of my top.

"How did it feel to put your cock inside me after all these years, Gunner?" I asked.

"Christ, Sage," he muttered as the camera began moving a lot. Based on what I could see, his eyes had dropped to his lap, so I assumed he was freeing himself from his pants. When the camera stopped moving and his eyes were focused on me again, he said, "I can't believe you're mine."

Smiling at him, I continued to touch my breast and promised, "Yes, baby, I'm all yours."

"Don't leave me here to do this myself," he demanded, his voice strained.

At his request, my hand slipped down my body and into my panties where I touched myself. "I'm so wet," I shared.

Gunner emitted a groan.

I didn't stop. "My fingers just aren't the same as yours. I wish you were here with me."

"I am, Sage. I'm right there with you. Can't you feel it? Can't you feel my hands touching you? Don't you feel my mouth on your body?"

The pace of my breaths had increased. "I do," I rasped. "And it makes me feel so good. I want you to feel just as good. Can you feel my mouth on your cock? Do you like the way my tongue glides along the length of it?"

"Fuck," he hissed. "Babe, I'm not going to last much longer."

I was happy he was close because I was right there with him. "Are you going to come for me, handsome?"

"Sage, are you close?"

"Come with me, Gunner."

And just like that, imagining my hands were Gunner's, I came apart watching him do the same. Through it all, his eyes never left mine.

CHAPTER 4

Gunner

OVER THE LAST WEEK AND A HALF, I LEARNED JUST HOW LITTLE patience I have when there is so much uncertainty in a given situation. The first of two hurricanes Sage was covering had hit the Carolina coast, and it had devastated the communities.

Thankfully, Sage had managed to come through on her promise to contact me each day. Getting that phone call was the only thing keeping me sane. I had been able to relax just a bit after I got her call following the first storm. I knew the worst of it had passed and she was okay, so that made me feel a lot better.

But the next storm, which was set to make landfall sometime within the next five or six hours, was the one I'd been dreading. Ever since I found out she was flying out there to cover these hurricanes, I hadn't stopped listening to all the reports. I learned more about hurricanes over the last week and a half than I had in my whole life. And with everything I learned, the biggest thing I discovered was that I didn't like them. Because I knew this monster storm had the potential to hurt Sage or worse… take her away from me permanently. The thought made me sick with worry.

"I wasn't going to say anything, Hayes, but now I'm concerned. You've been glued to that thing all day today. What's going on?"

That came from my co-worker, Trent Michaels. When I turned around, I found he wasn't alone. Another co-worker, Tyson Reed, was also with him.

Tyson added, "Yeah, do you have some beachfront property out there in North Carolina that you never told any of us about that you're worried about?"

I turned my attention back to the television in the break room at the Cunningham Security office and replied, "No."

"Okay, so you've suddenly decided you're fascinated by hurricanes then?" he pressed.

I shook my head. "It's her."

"Her?" Trent repeated. "Who?"

I lifted my hand, pointed to the television, and answered, "Her."

Tyson and Trent moved forward to stand beside me and watch the television, too. "Who's Sage Thompson?" Tyson asked.

Without taking my eyes off her, I declared, "The woman I'm in love with."

I didn't have to look away from her face to know that Tyson and Trent were no longer watching her. Their attention was entirely focused on me.

"Is this some kind of celebrity crush thing?" Tyson wondered.

"No."

"Since when have you been in love with some woman on television?" Trent asked.

"I've known her since I was in high school," I explained.

Trent pressed for more. "What happened?"

For the first time since I admitted the truth to them about Sage, I took my eyes from her and looked at Trent. "What do you mean?" I asked.

"You were with her in high school," he started. "That's where I met Delaney. And that's also where things started and ended with the two of us. Luckily, we've got another shot. What happened with you and this girl?"

I shook my head. "Nothing. I crushed on her for two years but never had the courage to ask her out. She ended up moving at the end of our junior year because her father's job transferred him to Oregon. I saw her for the first time since then on the news the night I got home from Tyson's party. I drove down to the news station that night."

Tyson put his hand on my shoulder and squeezed. "Brother, you have no idea how happy I am to hear this. And once I tell Quinn, she's going to be over the moon."

My eyes shot to his, and I sent him a questioning look.

He explained, "My woman has been nagging me about finding someone for you. In fact, the night of the party she mentioned it to me again. Now, I can go home and tell her she's off duty because you've got a girl."

"I'm thanking my lucky stars she came back to Windsor," I sighed. "She's the one. I have not a single doubt in my mind about it either."

"There's nothing like having a second chance," Trent insisted.

Nodding, I worried, "Yeah, but I just hope she gets back here safe. I've been glued to this channel for days now. If I don't hear from her, I can't sleep. Now I see her barely able to stand upright to even report on the next storm they're expecting because the wind is so strong, and all I want to do is fly out there and bring her back here myself."

The moment those words were out of my mouth, Trent and Tyson both turned their attention to the television again. They saw exactly what I was so concerned about with Sage. The hurricane that hit last week had just barely broken into the category three rank but weakened just before it made landfall and was downgraded to a category two. There was still plenty of destruction, and Sage had filled me in on just how horrible it had been.

But the bigger concern right now was the storm that was only hours away from her. It was well into the category four ranking, and there were no signs of the storm's strength subsiding.

"Damn," Tyson hissed.

I nodded my agreement. "Yep."

"I can't say I'd blame you if you did that," Trent noted. "Look how bad those winds are. And it hasn't even hit yet."

"I just need her to come home safe," I said.

"She will," Tyson insisted. "How long has she been out there?"

I looked at my friend and co-worker and replied, "Since the day after your party."

His brows pulled together. "I thought you said you reconnected the night of my party," he pointed out.

"We did. And then she was gone before I even woke up the next morning," I explained.

"Okay, but you said you've talked to her since she's been out there, right?" Trent asked.

It took me a second to figure out why they were asking all these questions, but I realized they were worried with the way I'd said it that perhaps I was hooked on a woman who had run off only hours after I'd reconnected with her.

I nodded and confirmed, "We've managed to talk at least

once a day." When I turned my attention back to the television, where Sage was still speaking into the camera, I confessed, "I'm afraid this storm is going to put an end to that, and I'm going to be stuck wondering if she's okay."

"You've got to have faith in her to know when it's time to seek shelter," Tyson started. "Obviously, I don't know her, but I would imagine she's good at her job or they wouldn't have sent her there to cover it."

I let out a laugh. "She said the same thing to me," I mumbled.

"Maybe you should trust her then," he suggested.

"I do. It's the storm's unpredictability that's making me uneasy," I explained.

Tyson gave my shoulder one last squeeze as he and Trent stood by my side until the end of Sage's segment. When it was finished, they walked out and left me alone with my thoughts. Sadly, none of them were good.

The wind howled as the rain battered the window of my hotel room.

In all my years as a meteorologist, I've never been caught in a hurricane like the one that was currently wreaking havoc on the North Carolina coastal towns. I was petrified. Not only for myself but also for everyone who was currently in the storm's path. Without even looking outside, I knew the residents of these communities were going to be rebuilding for years to come. One hurricane would have been devastating enough—it already had been—but a second one only days later would prove to be catastrophic.

My mind was whirling with a million thoughts. Before now, I hadn't ever felt this concerned about being on location for storm coverage. It was just something I did without giving it a second thought. I didn't know if my concern now was because this storm was as bad as it was, or if it was because I now had someone in my life that I really wanted to get home to.

At the same time, I couldn't imagine the worry going through his mind. Thankfully, I'd managed to talk to Gunner every day up until today. The hotel phones were no longer working and cell signal was spotty at best. I tried calling Gunner from my cell, but my phone would never call out. Knowing how much terror I'd heard in his voice each day I talked to him, I had no doubt he was losing his mind right now.

Jack, Dennis, and I had done all we could do earlier today. But we were now at a point where we simply needed to ride out the storm. When we first returned to the hotel hours ago, I hung with them in the lobby for a while. We ate dinner together but ultimately made our way to our rooms.

Now I was here forcing myself to listen to the sounds outside the hotel walls. I didn't imagine I'd ever need to do that, but I'd apparently become accustomed to listening to the wind. It had been howling for hours on end and had gotten to a point where I needed to think about it to hear it.

I didn't know if it would ever make its way to him, but I figured I'd send it anyway. In that moment, feeling the way I did, I wanted to talk to Gunner. Without a way to actually call, I decided to send him text messages letting him know how I was feeling.

Me: Hey. There's nothing I can do right now as we wait for the worst of the storm to pass. So, to occupy my mind, I'm going to 'talk' to you this way. I don't know if these messages will ever send. If they do, I'm apologizing in advance for what I expect could be a bunch of messages. So… I'm sorry.

Me: So, I guess I'll start by saying that I didn't think this was going to be bad. I mean, obviously, I'm a meteorologist. I knew what the models were showing for this storm. I knew it was mammoth and slow-moving. But, to be honest, this is the most terrifying experience of my life.

Me: I'll never complain about the snow again. It's nothing compared to this.

Me: I miss you, Gunner.

Me: A lot.

Me: I don't even notice the wind anymore unless I force myself to pay attention to it. Is that weird?

Me: I really wish I was home right now. I want you to come over to my place when I get back. If I were there right now, I'd want you curled up in my bed with me. Would you like that?

Me: You're the one keeping my mind from going crazy with a million bad thoughts right now. I hope you know how happy I am that I walked out of the news station and into your arms.

Me: The rain is hitting the building harder now. There's so much noise outside. I can't even describe how awful it sounds out there.

Me: I wish you were here with me.

Me: This is so scary.

Me: Handsome…

I didn't really know what else to say. There were a thousand things I could say, but I had a feeling Gunner was going to be fed up by the time all my messages went through. I decided to end them.

Me: I'll stop now. But please… I hope you're thinking about me. I can't wait to get home to you.

With that, I set my phone aside and curled up under the blanket. I tried to close my eyes and get some rest. It took a long time, but I eventually managed to fall asleep. And I was certain that was when the eye of the hurricane had settled over us, bringing a calm we hadn't had in hours.

It also meant we weren't out of the woods yet.

Three days later

I was exhausted.

I barely managed to get three hours of sleep the night of the second hurricane. And over the last couple of days, we'd been working long hours. Even though it had moved beyond us, I was still monitoring the path of the storm. Thankfully, it had weakened substantially and wouldn't bring any other state along the coast anywhere near the devastation it did to North Carolina.

That's precisely what had happened.

North Carolina was a disaster.

There was massive flooding, downed trees, power outages, and a general sense of dismay in the community.

Jack, Dennis, and I had been traveling all over trying to get a handle on the scope of the damage. It was truly shocking and overwhelming. And in so many situations, where we found people in need, we stepped up to help them. Each and every day had been physically demanding and exhausting.

And I think it was all beginning to take its toll on me.

I'd never had to cover back-to-back storms like this before. That, combined with the kind of storms they were, the fear they filled a person with, and the lack of sleep were the perfect cocktail for fatigue. To top it off, I still hadn't spoken to Gunner. I knew he must have been terrified, but there was nothing I could do to reach out to him.

Now, it was Saturday, and the only good news I had was that I was set to fly home. Flights had been grounded when the storm hit, but most of the airports were up and running again within forty-eight hours after it had passed.

Last night, I had gotten a decent amount of sleep, but I had a feeling the last two weeks had caught up with me. Despite how excited I was to finally go home, I had to drag myself out of bed this morning. It took everything in me not to climb back under the covers.

But we had a morning flight scheduled, so I couldn't give myself that extra time. After gathering my things, I left my hotel room and met the guys downstairs. Thankfully, they were ready to go.

We hadn't been on the road for more than five minutes when I began feeling nauseous. I made a noise from the passenger seat and Jack immediately looked over at me.

"Are you okay?" he asked.

I shook my head. "I feel awful. I thought I was just tired, but now I'm feeling nauseous," I replied. "I hope all that standing out in the rain didn't result in me getting the flu."

"Should we stop for something? We can get you something to eat to settle your stomach maybe," he suggested.

"I don't know," I admitted. "The thought of food makes me want to hurl."

"There's a bagel shop up here on the right," Dennis said from the back seat. "Let's stop quick and get something just in case you change your mind."

All I wanted to do was curl up in bed, but since that wasn't an option, I didn't care what we did. "Sure," I agreed.

We reached the bagel shop, and even though I didn't think I wanted anything, I figured it wouldn't hurt to have something plain to help later. The second we got inside, the smell of freshly baked bagels overwhelmed me. I looked to the guys and Dennis noted, "You don't look so good."

My eyes rounded, realizing I wasn't going to be able to hold it back. "Excuse me," I clipped as I pushed past them and ran toward the bathroom. Thankfully, it was unoccupied. As soon as I got the door shut, I dashed over to the toilet and vomited.

The entire time I was emptying my stomach, which had nothing in it to begin with, all I could think about was the fact that I didn't know how I'd be able to fly home feeling like this.

When I thought I had finished, I stood up and waited to leave. I wanted to give myself a minute to be sure I was okay. As if by some miracle, I realized I felt completely fine again. My eyes roamed the space as I took a few breaths until suddenly something caught my attention.

That's when my entire frame locked.

The sanitary product dispenser hung there on the wall, taunting me. Because I was late.

I was never late.

My cycle was like clockwork.

I walked backward, leaned my back against the wall, and took a few deep breaths.

Could I be pregnant?

Gunner and I used protection. I remembered seeing him put it on.

Except…

Except the last time he woke me up.

Suddenly, it all came back to me. He had been teasing me, and when I couldn't take it any longer, I took charge and climbed on top of him.

I knew I wouldn't be able to last the flight home without being able to confirm my suspicions, but I also didn't want to tell Jack and Dennis what was going on either. I hoped I'd be able to find a pregnancy test at the airport.

If not, it was going to be my first stop when I landed in Windsor.

And now, even though I'd missed Gunner terribly, I wasn't sure he'd be happy to hear this news.

The thought terrified me… even more than listening to the hurricane outside my room only a matter of days ago.

CHAPTER 5

Sage

When the plane touched down in Windsor roughly twenty minutes ago, I was ready to push myself through the crowd of people on board waiting to walk off the plane ahead of me.

Back in North Carolina, I had walked out of the bathroom in the bagel shop and found Jack and Dennis waiting for me with worried looks on their faces.

"Are you alright?" Jack asked.

I nodded. "Yeah, I think I'm better now," I assured him.

He held up a paper bag and said, "Figured it might help. I got you a plain bagel and had it toasted."

Truthfully, I didn't have much of an appetite, but I didn't think it was a wise idea not to have something. I smiled at Jack and thanked him as I took the bag from his hand. That bagel became my saving grace over the next few hours, too. Between the occasional bouts of nausea and the nerves I felt over the possibility of a pregnancy, my stomach was in knots. I'd slowly pulled off bits of the bagel and popped them into my mouth. They helped tremendously, and I managed to avoid getting sick again for the entire return flight.

Unfortunately, despite my best efforts, I wasn't able to find a pregnancy test in the airport. So, I spent the entire plane ride playing the night with Gunner over and over in my mind. To think it was possible we made a baby blew my mind. I wanted to be excited about it. But I didn't know how he'd react. We'd just barely gotten reacquainted with one another. This didn't exactly seem like the best way to start a relationship.

And the idea that Gunner might not want anything to do with me if this turned out like I had a feeling it would upset me.

But I wouldn't have to wonder for too much longer.

Because I'd finally managed to get off the plane. I said goodbye to Jack and Dennis and took off toward the long-term parking lot. And now that I was here, I wasn't interested in wasting any more time. I immediately pulled out of the lot and drove to the closest drug store. Inside, I picked out several different brands of tests because I wanted to be sure. Then I drove straight home.

Leaving everything else in my car, I grabbed the tests and my purse and ran into my house.

I climbed the stairs to my bedroom, tossed my purse down on the bed, and pulled out a box with one of the tests.

A minute later, I was pacing my bathroom. The instructions had said to wait a full three minutes to confirm the results, so I was doing the only thing I could do at that moment. I was pacing and panicking.

And in those minutes, I realized just how much I wanted the test to be positive. Of course, I didn't want anything to happen that would jeopardize what Gunner and I had started, but I also really wanted this to be for real.

I wasn't officially timing anything, but when I felt it had been close to three minutes, I walked back over to the sink. That's when I picked up the test and my heart started pounding. There were two blue lines on it, indicating I was, in fact, pregnant.

My free hand flew up to my mouth in shock as my eyes filled with tears.

Gunner and I had made a baby.

I didn't know how it was possible to be filled with such joy and terror all at the same time, but I was. The only way that was going to change was if I told Gunner. Until I knew how he felt about this, all I was going to feel was an overwhelming sense of dread.

I needed a plan. To give myself some time to think, I decided to take a shower. I turned on the water and hopped in, hoping I'd find some clarity there. Unfortunately, there wasn't any to be found. And I had a feeling the only way I was going to find some was by sharing the news with the man who needed to know.

As terrified as I was about what his reaction would be, I had to go to him.

So, I finished in the shower, dried my hair, and got dressed. Before I left, I pulled my phone out of my purse and saw that I had a bunch of text messages from Gunner and two voicemails. Seeing those stopped me in my tracks, and I sat down on the edge of my bed.

First, I noticed he responded to every single text I sent him.

Gunner: Hey back. Anytime you need to 'talk' to me, you do it. Never, ever apologize for that. I always want to hear whatever it is you need to say.

Gunner: You're smart. You know what to expect, and I have no doubts you'll use everything you know to keep yourself safe. I'm sorry you feel so terrified, but you should know that I think you're the bravest woman I've ever met.

Gunner: The snow can be fun. I agree with you. It's nothing compared to a hurricane.

Gunner: I miss you, too, Sage.

Gunner: More than just a lot.

Gunner: I don't think it's weird that you don't notice the wind anymore. It makes sense that if you've been hearing the same thing for a long time, it's going to be harder for it to stand out. That wind isn't like you, stranger. That's what it feels like every time I'm around you or talk to you or get your messages. It's like you're a stranger. But in a good way. I get to see all these new sides to you. And there isn't one of them that I don't like a whole lot.

Gunner: You have no idea how much I wish that you were here. And yes, as soon as I know you're back and you want me there, I'll curl up with you in your bed. Anytime you want that, Sage, I'll give it to you.

Gunner: Seeing your face and hearing your voice on the television has been the only thing that's kept me sane. I hope you know how happy I am that you knew who I was when you saw me and that your first instinct was to launch yourself into my arms.

Gunner: But even with all that's happening outside your hotel right now, you're safe inside, right?

Gunner: I wish I could have been there with you, too.

Gunner: I'm sorry you're scared. I'm scared, too.

Gunner: Babe...

Gunner: Don't ever stop. I'm always thinking of you. There hasn't been a moment since I woke up without you that morning that I haven't thought about you. I can't wait until you come back home to me, Sage.

My eyes were already filled with tears, but apparently,

that wasn't enough for me. I decided to listen to Gunner's voicemails.

"Sage, babe," he started, his voice sounding like he was struggling to speak. "It's the morning after the hurricane hit. I know you said you'd call me whenever you could, but I couldn't wait. I know there's probably no cell service, but I guess I was hoping I'd get lucky. I've seen the devastation out there, and it terrifies me. I'm not a very religious man, Sage, but I've been praying for you. I hope you're safe, baby. Please... please just call me as soon as you get this so I know you're okay."

I closed my eyes and the tears fell. The anguish in his voice was too much for me. If he sounded like that for the first message, I couldn't imagine what he sounded like in the second. I tapped on my screen and listened.

His voice was practically a whisper. He rasped, "It's me, Sage. It's been days. I haven't seen you on television, and you haven't called. You're supposed to be coming home tomorrow. If I don't hear from you by the end of the day, I'm flying out to North Carolina to bring you home myself. Please, honey, please find a way to call me."

I couldn't take it. I dropped my phone in my purse, grabbed the positive pregnancy test, the extra boxes I'd purchased, and ran through my house to my front door. Within seconds, I was in my car and driving to Gunner's house. I hoped I'd arrive and he'd be there.

Before I knew it, I'd made it to Gunner's place. I rang the doorbell and waited. It couldn't have been more than five seconds when the door opened. My tear-filled eyes connected with Gunner's tortured, sleep-deprived ones before he whispered, "Oh, thank God."

Gunner reached his hand out to my wrist, tugged me inside, and engulfed me in a hug. I didn't know if it was the shock of seeing him so torn up, the thought of what I had to share with him, the hormones from the pregnancy, or simply seeing him for the first time in two weeks, but I completely lost it.

The minute my cheek was resting against his chest, I burst into tears.

"Sage, baby," he rasped as he kept a firm hold on me.

"I missed you so much," I cried.

Gunner brought a hand up to my head and brushed my hair away from my face. He tucked the strands behind my ear before his thumb stroked over my cheek and wiped my tears away.

"Look at me, Sage," he urged.

I had barely just tipped my head back to look up at him when Gunner's lips touched mine. He gave me two slow, closed-mouth kisses before he pulled back and declared, "I love you."

I blinked my eyes in surprise.

"What?"

"Agony," he began. "I've been in agony these last few days. All those nights I spent talking to you up until the second storm, I had a pretty good feeling that what I felt for you was love. After going through these last couple of days, not knowing if you were okay and not having any way to reach you, I no longer have any doubts. And I didn't want to wait another minute to tell you how I feel."

My eyes searched his handsome face. "Say it again," I begged him.

He slowly grinned before he proclaimed softly, "I love you, Sage."

"I love you, too, Gunner," I returned, my voice just as soft. "And I promise you that I'm not just saying that because you said it to me. The day I left here and got on that plane, I knew it. Initially, I thought maybe it was just lust or because this was so new between us. But it didn't take me long to figure it out. I love the way you care about me. I love that you have no problem telling me exactly how you feel. And I love that you don't make me feel bad about being precisely who I am."

"What do you mean by that last statement?" he wondered.

I bit my lip and my eyes shifted to the side. That's when I realized I should have worded it differently. Because now I had to talk to him about this right to his face. It wasn't as easy as when there were a couple thousand miles and a phone screen between us.

"Sage?" he called.

"That first night I was in North Carolina," I started, snapping out of it. "You didn't let it get awkward when I decided to have a little bit of fun with you. I love that I feel like I can be myself, and you won't ever judge me for it."

"You can't possibly think that I'd ever judge you for that," he remarked. "Sage, that was one of the sexiest things I'd ever seen in my life, second only to when I had you naked in my bed. With everything you were saying to me that night, all it took was hearing that and seeing your beautiful face to get me to come."

I squeezed him around the waist and reminded him, "I was touching myself, too, handsome."

Gunner grinned. "Yeah. But I couldn't see any of that. And the little that I did see on the top half didn't really count because you had clothes on. You'll have to show me that again in person sometime."

The thought of doing that for him had me squirming. I shifted my weight back and forth on my feet as I squeezed my legs together.

"You know," he started. "Now that we're talking about it,

why wait? I've missed you. You've already admitted you missed me. That'll be the perfect way to reunite with each other."

Then Gunner took me by the hand and led me to his bedroom.

When we got there, he stopped at the foot of the bed, framed my face with his hands, and kissed me. One of his hands moved into my hair and cupped me behind the head while the other traveled down my body. Gunner's mouth moved from mine and he kissed me along my cheek until he was back at my ear. He whispered, "I loved thinking about you touching yourself, Sage. Now, I want to stop imagining it and see it for real."

Moments ago, when we'd been standing just inside the door to his place, it seemed like a great idea. Even with him kissing me and talking to me like he was, it was hard not to be turned on. But I suddenly realized that very soon I wouldn't look the same. And then Gunner might not ever want to see me doing that.

As if sensing the shift in my mood, Gunner pulled back and asked, "Is everything okay?"

I didn't know what to say. Technically, everything was okay. But I didn't know how Gunner would react, and that made it not okay.

So I shook my head.

I felt his body immediately tense. "What's wrong?"

"I have to tell you something, Gunner," I warned him.

"Okay. What is it?" he asked.

"But I don't want to tell you because I'm terrified that once I do, you'll walk away from me."

I wasn't sure how it was possible, but Gunner's body grew even more rigid. I hated what I was doing to him, but I wanted him to know how I felt before I just threw it out there.

"Sage, I'm not sure there's much you could tell me that would make me want to leave you," he asserted.

Looking up at him, feeling such worry consume my entire body, I rasped, "Okay, but you're saying that there might be some things I could tell you that would make it happen then, right? What are those things?"

He hesitated before he shrugged. "I don't know," he began. "I don't even really want to think about that. I mean, if you cheated on me…"

Suddenly, his hands let go of me and he took half a step back.

Then he questioned me. "Did you?"

I was completely stunned. He thought I cheated on him? My eyes were darting back and forth across his face as I tried to figure out why he would ever think that.

Apparently, my silence lasted too long and Gunner grew impatient. "Sage, did you let another man touch you while you were in North Carolina?"

"No," I cringed. "I can't even believe you think I'd do that."

He threw his hands out to the side and countered, "Well, you're telling me that you think I'm going to leave you, and you aren't saying why you feel that way. That makes me think it's got to be the absolute worst possible thing. What do you expect me to think?"

"Not that," I mumbled, looking down at the ground.

After a beat of silence, Gunner called my name. "Sage?"

I lifted my gaze to meet his. My emotions were running wild, my heart was pounding, and I was certain my lungs had stopped working.

Gunner gently encouraged me. "Whatever it is, honey, we'll work it out. I promise you. As long as you love me and I love you, there's nothing we can't work through."

I nervously bit my lip.

"I wasn't sure if I was going to make my flight this morning," I blurted.

His brows pulled together, obviously confused.

"After spending so much time over the last week or so out in the cold and the rain plus not really sleeping well, I could barely get out of bed this morning. I'd been feeling pretty sluggish ever since the night of the second storm. Anyway, we left the hotel this morning and I felt awful. Jack was driving us to the airport and decided to stop at a bagel shop that was on the way since we hadn't had any breakfast—"

"I told you not to do that to yourself," Gunner scolded me.

Nodding, I assured him, "I know. But this wasn't about that. As soon as I walked inside the shop, I felt sick and had to run to the bathroom."

Gunner went from being irritated that I hadn't had breakfast to being genuinely concerned. I knew this because he looked me up and down as though he were trying to assess whether or not I was actually okay.

"I got sick and threw up," I shared.

His eyes widened.

"I'm sorry," I lamented. "I know this is probably not the reunion you were expecting."

"I don't understand, Sage. First, are you okay? And second, why would you getting sick make me want to leave you?"

I closed my eyes and took a deep breath. "I love you," I whispered. When I opened my eyes again, I stared into Gunner's eyes and informed him, "I wasn't actually sick."

His head jerked back. "But you just said you threw up," he noted.

Nodding, I explained, "That's because I'm pregnant."

And with those four words, I knew I had rocked Gunner's world.

CHAPTER 6

Sage

I WATCHED AS GUNNER'S LEGS GAVE OUT FROM UNDER HIM. Thankfully, he was standing right in front of the bed and landed on the edge of it as his hands went to his thighs, just above his knees.

"Gunner, please say something," I begged after too much time had passed without so much as a grunt or a gasp from him.

I looked down to see his fingers gripping his legs tight. His breathing had gotten shallow, and I worried that I was making him even more stressed by standing there. Thinking that he might have needed some time to himself, I rasped, "I'll give you some time."

But just as I was about to walk away, his head snapped up and his hand shot out to my hip. "Don't go."

I didn't move.

Instead, I waited for him to give me some indication of what he was thinking. There was a small part of me that felt the tiniest bit of relief that he hadn't wanted me to leave. I couldn't help but think that was a good thing.

As good as I thought that was, I had to admit I felt like I was dying inside. It had been minutes since I told Gunner I was pregnant, and he hadn't said anything about it. I would have been lying if I said my heart wasn't pounding and for all the wrong reasons, too.

Finally, after what felt like a lifetime, Gunner brought his other hand up to my opposite hip. His hands rested there as he looked up at me and asked, "We made a baby?"

Tears instantly streamed down my cheeks as I nodded and confirmed, "Yes."

He swallowed hard, but never took his eyes off mine.

Unable to control myself, I thought it was best to do some explaining. So, I apologized, "I'm sorry. It was my fault. I've been trying to figure it out all day and I realized that it happened when you woke me up in the middle of the night. I was too caught up in everything, not thinking, and—"

I stopped speaking the moment he squeezed my hips and rested his head on my abdomen. One of his hands drifted around to my lower back while the other slid down right next to his face. With his palm pressed flat against my belly, Gunner kissed me there.

"We made a baby, Sage. Why are you apologizing to me?"

I brought a hand to the top of his head and explained, "I'm nervous. I don't want you to be upset with me."

"I'm just as responsible for this as you are," he remarked.

"Is that... are you okay with that?" I asked.

"I find it astounding that you even think that's a question that should be asked," he stated as he pulled his head away from my body and looked up at me again.

Still unsure of his mindset, I said, "I'm not trying to suggest that you wouldn't be responsible, Gunner. It's just that... I don't think either of us expected this. I'm not sure there are many people who plan to get pregnant with someone the first time they're together intimately."

"Are you upset?" he wondered.

"I'm upset that I don't exactly know how you feel about this pregnancy," I shared.

"How do *you* feel about it?"

Staring down at him at that moment, he looked completely vulnerable. If I was a bad person I could have easily crushed him with my words. But that wasn't who I was. So, I answered honestly, "I was shocked at first. But I've had some time to come to terms with it. And I'm really excited about it. To tell you the truth, I don't think I could be happier about the fact that we made this little miracle."

The tension left Gunner's body right before he leaned forward and pressed a kiss to my belly again. He kept his palm flat against me and continued to kiss. Eventually, though, he pulled back just far enough so he could speak to me.

"Next to hearing you tell me that you love me, Sage, there's nothing better you could have shared with me," he said.

The relief I felt in that moment was indescribable. So much so that I couldn't stop myself from sagging into him. Gunner took my weight and settled me on his lap. I simply wrapped my arms around his neck and held on to him as the sandals that were on my feet fell to the floor.

With his hand running up and down my back, Gunner asked, "Why do you think I would ever walk away from you over something like this, Sage?"

I pulled back to look at him. When our eyes were locked on one another, I explained, "It's like I said before. This isn't exactly the kind of thing that most people plan for after being with someone for the first time. I mean, we weren't even officially dating, Gunner."

"So, you think that I'd get a free pass and you'd be saddled with the responsibility on your own?" he pressed.

I hadn't been trying to insinuate that he'd be that kind of guy, but I could understand why he'd think that. What I loved, though, was knowing how much it bothered him that I might have thought it was even a possibility. Because even though we hadn't planned for this baby, it told me that I didn't exactly make a mistake. Gunner clearly wanted to step up to the plate.

"What do you want me to say?" I asked. "I was anxious about it because I had no idea where you stood. We literally saw each other for the first time in twenty years, and only hours into it we made a baby. I didn't know what to expect when I told you, but I'm happy that you want to be responsible for your child."

Gunner's eyes searched my face adoringly. Then they slowly drifted down my body. With one hand resting lightly on my thigh, Gunner said softly, "I think you're going to be the most beautiful pregnant woman that's ever walked the face of this earth. I can't wait to see our baby growing inside you."

His hand drifted up my thigh to my belly. It stopped there momentarily before moving farther up my torso. He cupped my breast and whispered in my ear, "I missed you, Sage. More than I could even begin to tell you."

As his thumb moved back and forth over my breast, I rasped, "You don't have to explain it, Gunner. I already know because I felt the exact same way about you."

He smiled at me and continued to stroke with his thumb. I was squirming in his lap. Feeling the evidence of his arousal under me, knowing how long it had been for the both of us, I begged, "Make love to me, handsome."

Gunner let out a little laugh and asked, "Do you know that you said that same thing to me two weeks ago?"

Biting my lip, I nodded. "And I don't regret it in the least," I assured him.

With that, Gunner leaned forward and captured my mouth with his. He kissed me for a long time, continuing to rub my nipple through the fabric of my shirt, until he could stand it no longer. Pulling his mouth from mine, Gunner's hands went to the hem of my shirt and tore it over my head. His lips touched the skin at my collarbone as he worked behind my back to unclasp my bra.

All I could do was relish the feel of having his hands on me again for the first time in two weeks. He gently slid the straps of my bra from my shoulders and down my arms. Then, he slipped one hand under my knees and the other behind my back before he stood and carried me over to the side of the bed. Gunner set me down in the bed, but did it with such care and concern, I felt myself getting emotional.

He put a knee to the bed, climbed in, and lifted his shirt over his head. After tossing it aside, Gunner pulled off the rest of my clothing. Then he wasted no time showing me how much he missed me.

His mouth ran over every inch of my skin.

Licking.

Kissing.

Tasting.

Nipping.

His hands were everywhere, and his attention was entirely focused on making me feel good. He did it all, and somehow still managed to remove his pants.

When he slid inside me, it was all about demonstrating his love for me. Not only could I feel it with every touch of his hands, kiss of his lips, or stroke of his hardened length inside me, but it was also in the words he whispered.

Missed you so much, Sage.

So sweet. So beautiful.

How'd I get so lucky?

Would have waited another twenty years if I knew I was going to get you in the end.

I was caught up, so caught up, in everything he was doing. His touch was so tender, and his movements were gentle. While I didn't think he was holding himself back in the least, the way he was touching me made me feel like I was precious to him. I could feel just how much this meant to him, how much I meant to him.

This was the utter definition of making love.

I knew it. I had the proof.

It was Gunner and the way he used every part of his body to reconnect with mine. Never had I ever experienced something so beautiful in my life than when I was in bed with Gunner. I'd experienced the same feeling the first night we were together. I knew it now. I just hadn't realized it then because I'd been so caught up in seeing him again after so many years.

But this was it.

And because I didn't want to miss a moment of it, I lost myself completely in him. Once I'd done that, it didn't take long for me to end up at the point of no return, breathless and desperate for release.

"Come for me, Sage," Gunner pleaded.

I couldn't stop myself. Everything he'd done up to that point, everything he was continuing to do, and the urgency in his tone sent me soaring.

I cried out softly and surrendered myself to all that I was feeling, physically and emotionally.

Somehow, though I was consumed by my own pleasure, I was unable to miss that somewhere in the middle of it, Gunner had found his own. I forced myself to pay attention to it and had no regrets about it.

The sight of him and the sounds that escaped from somewhere deep inside him stole my breath.

Post-orgasm bliss was a beautiful place to be. Gunner and I both basked in it for a while without any words. A minute or two after Gunner had pulled out and fallen to his back, I sat up and said, "I'm going to run and clean up."

He dipped his chin.

Then he watched intently as I made my way around the foot of the bed and across the room. I loved the feeling of having his eyes on me.

After I returned from the bathroom, Gunner and I were cuddled up in his bed. I didn't plan on staying the night, but I wasn't ready to leave just yet either. On top of that, I didn't want to sleep without Gunner tonight.

"Will you follow me back to my place later?" I asked.

"Everything okay?" he wondered.

"Yeah. I just… I kind of want to sleep in my bed after spending so many nights in a hotel, but I don't want to sleep without your arms around me tonight."

"Anything you want," he declared. "But I'm not going to follow you there. I'll drive you there in my truck. We'll come back and get your car tomorrow or something."

"That works for me," I agreed.

At that, Gunner and I fell into a comfortable silence. Between the lack of sleep from my trip out to the east coast and now a pregnancy to contend with, I was exhausted. That combined with the warmth of Gunner's body had me nearly asleep when he suddenly spoke.

"I'm not looking to just be responsible, Sage," Gunner stated.

I opened my eyes and lifted my cheek from his chest to look at him. "What?" I asked.

"With this baby," he started. "I want to be more than just a sperm donor and financial provider. It's important to me."

"I never thought of you as that," I asserted. "I work and make my own money, Gunner. I'm not looking for your financial support. When it comes to the baby, I want you to be involved as much as you want to be."

His thumb stroked along my cheekbone briefly before he lamented, "I'm sorry. I didn't mean to imply that you were after my money. I know you're a very capable woman. But I was raised by a single mom. I don't want that for my child."

It hit me then how quickly this whole thing between Gunner and I had moved. I didn't even know things like this about him. He came from a single-parent home. I had no idea what that was like for him or how it was going to impact him moving forward.

"I had no idea," I said.

"I know. I'm not upset about that. I just want you to know that I don't have it in me not to be involved. Aside from staying true to the promise I made to myself years ago, I love you. I'd never want you to have to do this on your own."

My head dipped to one side. "What did you promise yourself?" I asked.

After giving me a gentle squeeze, Gunner shared, "That if I made the choice to have a family, I'd never abandon them the way my father abandoned my mom and me."

Hearing those words made my heart hurt. It was such a bittersweet sentiment. I loved that he felt a sense of obligation and responsibility to his baby, but it hurt my heart to know that he'd endured a life without his own father.

"How old were you when he left?" I asked.

"He left her before I was even born," he replied.

"You never met him."

Gunner shook his head.

"Was it hard for you and your mom?"

He gave me a noncommittal look. "It wasn't easy, but it could have been much worse. My mom worked her tail off to provide for us. She never let me see it, but I figured it out on my own. When I realized how much she was sacrificing and doing without just so I could have more, I put a stop to it. She never knew that I saw how bad things were for her."

"I'm sorry that you both went through something so difficult," I apologized. "It hurts my heart to think you had to struggle like that."

Gunner's hand came up to my head, where he ran his fingers through my hair. "I appreciate that, babe. But I'm okay. We did alright for ourselves; we're both happy now. She's got a good man in her life now, and she deserves to have that."

I gave him a nod before dropping my cheek back to his chest. Gunner continued to run his fingers through my hair. I could have easily fallen asleep with him doing that, but something he said kept running through my mind.

"You didn't make the choice, handsome," I stated.

"Pardon?"

"You said that your promise to yourself was that if you ever made the choice to have a family, you'd never abandon them the way your father did," I clarified. "I'm just saying that you didn't exactly make that choice in our situation."

Gunner didn't respond. At least, not immediately.

Following several beats of silence, he ordered, "Sage, look at me."

I lifted my head again and turned my attention to him.

Once my gaze was on him, he assured me, "I made a choice. When I saw you on my television screen that night I drove down to the news station, I knew you were going to be someone special in my life. And I wanted that. I wanted whatever it was that having you meant. Bringing you back here that night and making love to you was a choice. Maybe we didn't exactly plan this and got caught up in the moment, but I'm not upset that the choice we made together led to us making a baby. I don't ever want you to think that I'm here out of obligation. I'm here because I chose you."

He was perfect. Gunner was the perfect man. And I considered myself to be pretty lucky to be the woman he chose. So lucky, I thought it prudent to brag a bit.

"Walking out of work that night and into your arms was the best thing that could have happened to me. I'm beginning to think I couldn't have chosen a better man to get caught up in the moment with. And I think you're going to be the best daddy to have ever walked the face of this earth."

"Fuck," he breathed.

"What?" I asked, tensing up.

"I'm going to be a dad."

I beamed at him. "Yeah, you are."

"And you're going to be a mom, Sage," he noted.

A mom.

I was going to be a mom.

I had no idea what I was doing. Neither of us did. But I knew that as long as I had Gunner by my side and we loved each other, we'd figure it out together.

I didn't respond to his statement. Instead, I dropped my cheek to his chest again and just allowed myself to be happy that I'd finally found something that I was beginning to think I wouldn't ever have.

After some time had passed, Gunner asked, "Are you tired?"

"Exhausted."

"Come on, then. Let me get you home and in your bed," he urged.

"Okay."

With that, Gunner and I got dressed. Then he took me home and wrapped me in his arms in my bed.

And that night, even though my entire life had changed forever in a matter of hours, I fell asleep feeling happier than I had been in a really long time. It was all thanks to one man.

CHAPTER 7

Sage
Four weeks later

"I CAN'T BELIEVE WE'RE GOING TO SEE THE BABY FOR THE FIRST time today," I bubbled, practically bouncing out of my seat.

"And we'll hear the heartbeat, right?" Gunner asked.

Nodding, I confirmed, "Yes, that's what they told me. I think that's what's going to make this feel like it's really happening. I'm so excited."

Gunner reached across the center console and curled his fingers around mine. "Me too," he shared.

It was Monday afternoon, just over four weeks since I returned from North Carolina and found out that I was pregnant, and Gunner and I were on our way to our first official appointment for the baby.

Even though I had the positive store-bought pregnancy tests, when I called my OB/GYN the Monday after I returned from my work trip, he sent me to get bloodwork done to confirm the pregnancy. I had that done on Tuesday morning and received a call that afternoon that I needed to get scheduled for my first appointment because I was, in fact, pregnant.

The last couple of weeks had been a real eye-opener

for the both of us. I'd been sick every day, and it was awful. I'd wake up because I was feeling nauseous. The first night Gunner stayed at my place, he woke up to find me bent over the toilet. If he was repulsed by it, he didn't let on. In fact, he stayed there with me, holding my hair away from my face and rubbing his hand up and down my back.

While I found that my symptoms improved as the day progressed, I mostly felt pretty bad. The only thing I'd been able to work out so far was that I only ever vomited first thing in the morning. It made me feel marginally better, but the waves of nausea lasted until late afternoon.

My level of exhaustion was immeasurable. I couldn't even begin to comprehend just how tired I felt all the time.

Work was tough. I wasn't looking to share the news just yet since it was so early, but it was difficult not to say something. I almost wanted to apologize to my co-workers for my lack of enthusiasm. The truth was that I could barely keep my eyes open. When I came home after a long shift, I immediately curled up on the couch and took a nap.

Gunner had been spending nearly all of his free time with me, even though I spent most of that time either sleeping or feeling sick. There were moments when I felt better than others, so I did my best to take advantage of them. I didn't experience them nearly as often as I would have liked, so it made me appreciate them that much more.

One of those moments was right now. I felt pretty good, all things considered. I had been scheduled to be off from work, so I didn't need to worry about that. Gunner insisted on going to the appointment with me, so he left work early and picked me up at home a few minutes ago.

"I feel like I have a thousand questions, but I don't know where to start with all of them," I admitted.

"We'll get all your questions answered, Sage," Gunner started. "Besides, I'm sure the doctor is going to have an idea about some of your concerns anyway. I'm guessing a lot of women have some of the same questions about their pregnancies. No matter what, we won't leave until you're comfortable with everything."

"Okay," I said, feeling myself relax a bit.

Gunner gave my hand a squeeze, and I realized just how thankful I was that he made such a big deal about coming with me.

"Thank you," I murmured after he pulled into the lot and parked his truck.

"For what, stranger?" he asked, turning his attention to me.

"For insisting on being here with me," I shared, ignoring the fact that he'd come up with such a unique endearment and had started using it more frequently with me. "It's the first appointment, and I don't know what to expect. I feel better that you're here with me for this one."

"I'm going to be here for every appointment, Sage. Not just this one. You aren't doing any of this alone," he insisted.

I leaned over the console and pressed a kiss to his lips. "I love you, handsome."

"Love you, too."

"Ready?" I asked.

He gave me a nod and instructed, "Wait for me to come around and open your door."

"Okay."

With that, Gunner exited the truck and came around to open my door.

Twenty-five minutes later, I was sitting on a table in the exam room wearing a fancy gown. I'd already filled out a battery of paperwork and had had my weight and blood pressure assessed. I also had to pee in a cup. That was one of those things I didn't seem to have any problems doing these days. I thought it was only at the end of the pregnancy when a baby was sitting on my bladder that I'd be dealing with such an inconvenience, but apparently, I had it all wrong.

The door opened and the man I assumed was Dr. Perry walked in.

"Sage?" he asked.

Nodding, I replied, "That's me."

He extended his hand to me, shook mine, and introduced himself. "Dr. Perry. It's nice to meet you."

"You, too," I returned.

Before I could say anything else, he looked to Gunner and asked, "Is this dad?"

"Yes, sir," Gunner answered, evidently very proud of his new title. "Gunner Hayes."

"Pleasure to meet you," Dr. Perry said. "Alright, so I'm sure you have a lot of questions. Why don't you start and let me know if there are any overwhelming concerns you have?"

"Um, I'm not sure there's anything that's really overwhelming. It's probably all pretty standard—" I got out before I was cut off.

"She's really sick," Gunner interrupted. "Every day. She's up vomiting every morning. And she feels sick nearly all day long. We know women can be sick during pregnancy, but is this normal?"

"Some nausea and vomiting is normal. In fact, it's been said that the sicker you are, the healthier the pregnancy. Now, if it's causing you to lose weight or you can't keep anything down, then we'll need to talk about that a bit more because it could be an indication of a more serious condition."

"I'm able to eat," I chimed in. "And I've only been vomiting in the morning before I've had anything to eat. The nausea gets better as the day progresses. I was looking for some relief and read about ginger, but I'm not a fan of it. Are there any other options?"

"The fact that you're able to keep food down is a good sign," Dr. Perry confirmed. "We'll talk a bit more about your diet in a little bit, but preliminarily, my recommendation is that you try to eat something every hour. Not a full meal, obviously. But high-quality, lean protein food choices are a good idea. Half a stick of string cheese or a few almonds. Some women have success with ginger, but not all. Most women see the sickness subside once they're out of the first trimester. If you're one of the lucky ones, you're almost there."

I turned my attention to Gunner and noted, "The sicker I am, the healthier the pregnancy. You're going to need to keep that in mind so you don't make yourself crazy."

Gunner let out a laugh as he shook his head.

Dr. Perry said, "How about you let me give you a quick rundown of what's going to happen here today?"

"That works."

With that, Dr. Perry explained everything that I could expect for the appointment. He went on to perform a routine gynecological exam. Gunner stayed in the room with me, but I wondered how comfortable he was sitting there through that.

After the physical exam, they got me set up for the ultrasound. Dr. Perry continued to answer all my questions. Gunner even threw out a few of them. Most of his questions were all about what I should and shouldn't be doing and whether it was okay for me to continue working a normal work schedule.

Once Dr. Perry had answered all our questions, the technician came in and explained the procedure for the ultrasound before she went ahead with anything. I was so excited to finally see the baby, I would have agreed to just about anything.

Minutes later, with the lights dimmed, the technician inserted the wand and we saw a black and white image appear on the screen. I wasn't sure Gunner or I knew what we were looking at, so we waited patiently for an explanation.

Thankfully, we didn't have to wait too long.

Pointing at a black circle on the screen, she said, "So this right here is the gestational sac. And if you look closely at the white spot inside, you can see your baby."

Gunner reached out to hold my hand.

"Wow," I marveled. "That's the most amazing thing I've ever seen."

"Let me just get a few measurements real quick and then I'll show you something else even more amazing," the technician stated.

Gunner's fingers tightened. He was resting his elbows on the edge of the exam table holding my hand up so the back of it was right in front of his mouth. I felt his lips pressing kisses to the back of my hand, and I couldn't resist. While the technician took the measurements, I turned my head away from the screen and looked at Gunner. He had been staring at the screen, but when he noticed my movement, his eyes came to mine.

I could feel the love coming from him in just the look he gave me. Gunner was head over heels in love. With me, for sure. But with this baby, without a doubt.

"Okay," the technician interrupted our moment. "If you look here, you should be able to see this little flutter. Do you see that?"

"Yeah," Gunner and I responded in unison.

She said, "That's your baby's heart beating. Do you want to hear it?"

I nodded as I felt Gunner's hand tense.

The ultrasound tech pushed a couple buttons, and suddenly, the room filled with the sound of our baby's heartbeat. My free hand flew up and covered my mouth. Tears filled my eyes as I looked back at Gunner.

I immediately noticed his eyes were wet.

"That's our baby," I cried.

Gunner kept one hand holding mine while his other one came to my forehead. "That's our baby," he repeated, his voice husky.

I didn't know if I was moved more by hearing our baby's heartbeat for the first time or seeing Gunner's reaction to it.

"It's beautiful," I rasped.

"The heart rate is really good, too. It's at one forty-eight," she announced.

The technician took a few more measurements, printed a bunch of ultrasound pictures, and gave a few of them to us. "I'm going to step out now, but Dr. Perry should be back in shortly to speak with you."

"Thank you," we replied.

"You're welcome. Oh, and in case you were wondering, your due date is June twelfth," she shared.

"June twelfth?" I asked.

"Yes."

After I gave her a nod, she left.

Gunner and I were alone for the first time since before Dr. Perry had originally walked in. I had a million things I wanted to say to Gunner, but I wanted to wait for his reaction.

No sooner did the technician walk out when he declared, "We're moving in together."

I shook my head in surprise. "What?"

His head moved back and forth slowly as his eyes got wet again. "Sage, baby, I don't want to miss a moment of this pregnancy. I love you. I want to be with you. And I want to be there for all the moments like this," he explained.

Looking away, I tried to process the unexpected reaction. "Gunner… I—"

"Please, Sage," he interrupted. His voice sounded so pained, it forced me to look at him. And when I did, I saw the despair in his face. "I promise I won't push for anything else right now, but I want this. Please don't stop me from having this experience," he begged.

He felt so strongly about it, and I knew I should have considered myself lucky. So, I did the only thing I could. I lifted a hand to cup the side of his face and agreed, "Okay, handsome. We can move in together."

I saw the tension physically leave him, and his body relaxed. "Thank you," he sighed. "I love you so much, Sage."

"Then you should kiss me," I ordered.

Gunner brought his lips to mine and kissed me. After he did, I pulled back just a touch and breathed, "I love you, too."

Just then, there was a knock at the door. Dr. Perry came in with a file in his hand. He was looking through it and said, "Alright, so everything looks great on the ultrasound. All the measurements are good, we've got a June due date, and there's a solid heart rate. I know we talked about a lot of things earlier when we were doing the exam, but have either of you had any additional questions come to mind now that you've had a little more time?"

I looked to Gunner before looking back at Dr. Perry. "No, I think we've got it all covered now," I said.

"I have a question," Gunner said.

My brows pulled together in confusion. We had literally discussed so many things already, I couldn't imagine what else had popped into his head.

"Sure," Dr. Perry replied.

Gunner looked at me, grinned, and turned his attention back to Dr. Perry. "From a standpoint of safety when it comes to sex, is there anything that would be off-limits?"

"Gunner!" I gasped.

He looked at me and shrugged. "What?" he countered. "It's a valid question."

Dr. Perry chuckled and insisted, "It's actually a more common question than you might think, Sage. And the answer to that is that you can continue to do whatever is comfortable for the both of you. The baby is protected by the cervix, so nothing you do during sex will harm him or her. Sage's pregnancy is healthy, so there's nothing at this point that would make me tell you to refrain from intimacy."

Seemingly proud of himself, Gunner thanked Dr. Perry. I had a feeling it had little to do with the exam and results and more to do with the permission to have sex.

After going over a few more things with us, Dr. Perry excused himself so I could get dressed. The minute the door closed behind the doctor, I gave Gunner a death glare.

"What's that look about?" he asked.

I opened my mouth to answer him but couldn't find the words, so I snapped my mouth shut and shook my head at him instead. Finally, I scolded him, "I can't believe you asked him about having sex!"

"Why? He said it was a common question," Gunner defended himself.

"Yeah, but we've had sex since we found out I was pregnant," I reminded him.

Gunner nodded. "I know. But if you'll recall, it's been very tame," he noted.

"And?"

"And that's why I asked Dr. Perry if anything was off-limits," he returned. "I figured that was the best way to put it."

"The best way?" I repeated.

Raising his eyebrows in disbelief, Gunner asked, "Would you have preferred it if I'd given him details? I mean, I could have just said, 'Hey, doc, I knocked up my woman the first night we had sex, which was incidentally, the first night we'd seen each other in about twenty years. She went away for work for two weeks after that, so I haven't really had a chance to do everything I want to do to her just yet. Is it cool if we experiment with different positions now that she's pregnant?'"

My lips parted in shock. "That would have been so much worse," I declared. "He probably would have judged me for giving it up on the first date."

"If he thought anything," Gunner began as he walked toward me. "He would have thought I was one lucky man. He would not have been thinking anything else about you."

I rolled my eyes at him and finished getting dressed. Once I had my clothes back on, Gunner walked up behind me and wrapped his arms around me.

"Are you mad at me?" he asked as he kissed the skin at my neck.

I was certain he'd already figured out what kissing me there did to me. He knew exactly what he was doing.

I leaned my body back into his chest and answered softly, "No, Gunner. I'm not mad at you."

He pressed one more kiss to my neck, quickly walked around the front of me, and sat in the chair that was right there. Then he put his hands to my hips and spoke to my belly.

"Do you hear that, baby? I won our first argument. Mommy's not mad at me."

I wanted to tell him that he hadn't won our first argument because I was stubborn like that, but he was talking to our baby. I couldn't possibly ruin that moment. Instead, I decided to sweeten it by putting my hand to the top of his head when he leaned forward and kissed my belly.

"Love you, baby," he whispered there.

Then he stood and kissed me. "Love you, Sage."

"I love you, too."

"Let's go make the rest of your appointments so we can get out of here and go pack up my place," he instructed as he put an arm around my shoulders.

"Pack up your place?" I asked, looking up at him.

Gunner nodded and wondered, "Did you already forget that we decided to move in together?"

"No, I just didn't think you meant today," I explained. "And I didn't know that we'd decided to move to my place."

"Oh. Well, I meant today," he returned. "And for the record, us going to pack up my place really just means that you're going to sit and watch while I pack up some things. We'll figure out the rest later. If we want to bring any of the bigger furniture I have over, I'll get a couple of the guys to help me out. As for your place being the place we move into, it just makes sense. I'm in a condo, you're in a house. You have the space for the baby's room and then some. I have it, but the room isn't as big. Your place has a yard; mine does not. There's privacy at your place and not nearly that much at mine. Is that enough reasons or do you want more?"

I smiled and insisted, "That's enough reasons."

With that, Gunner gave me a kiss on the forehead and said, "Good."

Then, we went out and made my appointments before Gunner drove us back to his place so he could pack it up while I watched. And as I sat there watching him do it, all I could think was how fast everything was moving and how much I didn't mind it at all.

CHAPTER 8

Gunner

IT AMAZED ME TO THINK HOW MUCH MY LIFE HAD CHANGED IN JUST a few short weeks. It had been just a couple days shy of two months since Sage and I reconnected, and barring the uncertainty and worry I experienced when she was in North Carolina for work those two weeks, it had been the best two months of my life.

I thought back to the day of Tyson's party. The low I felt walking through my front door that night was a distant memory. I almost couldn't remember how awful I'd been feeling, thinking I'd somehow missed my shot at finding happiness.

But I hadn't.

Because now I had her and the family we were starting.

That was a whole other thing. When the day rolled around that Sage was supposed to be returning from reporting on the hurricanes, I had been such a mess. Having not heard from her in days, I was thinking the absolute worst had happened. So, I never expected to open my door and see her standing there, let alone have her tell me that she was pregnant.

In that instant, everything changed.

Two months before that, I was finding myself feeling rather depressed. Then, she showed up on the television, and I knew I had to take that chance. It was the best decision of my life because the second she launched herself into my arms that night, I knew nothing was ever going to be the same for me anymore.

It had been two weeks since Sage's first doctor's appointment, and we were just over a week away from Thanksgiving. I had officially moved into Sage's house the same day as our appointment, and over the next couple of days, we brought a few extra pieces from my place. My ultimate plans included being able to ask Sage to marry me, but I thought it might be too much too soon for her. She was going through a lot right now, and I didn't want to add any stress to her life.

So, for the time being, I was going to hang on to my place. I didn't want to officially list it for sale until the two of us had more time together. While I was sure about us, I didn't want to be stupid either. We were going to be going through a lot of changes over the next several months. I wanted the two of us to get through a few disagreements with Sage realizing that no matter what was happening, we'd always find a way to work through it.

And I believed that our current living arrangement would help the both of us with that tremendously.

So, I talked to my realtor and mentioned that I was looking to sell in the next few months. I explained that I didn't want to officially list it, but that if there was a buyer who'd be a perfect fit, I'd consider bringing it up to Sage.

For now, all I wanted to do was enjoy my time with her.

I had just left work a few minutes ago and was heading home. Sage's schedule was a bit unique, and essentially it worked on a two-week cycle. She didn't work typical Monday through Friday hours. She'd work Monday and Tuesday, have off on Wednesday and Thursday, and then work Friday,

Saturday, and Sunday. Then the next week, she'd only work on Wednesday and Thursday.

This week was a Wednesday and Thursday week only. Since today was Monday, I was looking forward to getting home and seeing her.

But much to my surprise, I pulled into the driveway to find that her car wasn't there. Admittedly, I was a bit disappointed. Because even though Sage and I were living together, Sage hadn't mentioned going anywhere. But I was quickly learning never to make assumptions about anything with her. She'd proven to me that she was a woman of many surprises. I never knew what to expect with her and actually enjoyed seeing her in all these different ways.

After I parked and got out, I let myself into the house. I did a quick walk-through but didn't notice anything out of place.

I decided to give her a call. The phone rang three times before I was greeted by her.

"Did you just get back home?" she asked, sounding disappointed.

"Um, yeah. Is that okay?" I wondered.

She let out a frustrated groan but answered, "Yeah. I was just hoping I'd get back there before you. I got the itch to do something today. And when I looked at the time, I thought for sure that there was plenty of it left before you'd be back. Obviously, I was wrong."

"What did you get the itch to do?" I asked.

"Oh, well, I'm almost there," she started. "I'll just show you all the excitement I have planned for us when I get there. I'm actually going to need your help carrying everything, though. So, if you don't mind, I'd really appreciate it if you could meet me outside in about two minutes."

"Of course. What did you buy?" I pressed her for an answer.

"You'll see when I get there," she insisted. "Just meet me outside."

With that, Sage disconnected the call. I couldn't even begin to imagine what she was up to now. This was precisely the type of thing that I loved about her. I would think things were going one way, and she'd suddenly do something to stir it up. It was like the first night she was out in North Carolina and decided to have video chat phone sex with me. I *never* expected that from her. But now that she'd put it out there, I was happy to know that it was something we'd be able to do in the future if she had to go on another work trip.

A minute later, I walked outside and met Sage just as she was pulling into the driveway. Through the windshield, I could see she had a big smile on her face. Seeing that made my day. I wouldn't have cared what she bought or had up her sleeve. If it was making her that happy, it wasn't going to be a problem for me.

I opened her door and gave her a kiss. "Hey, stranger. Did you have a good day?"

Bobbing her head up and down, she bubbled, "The best." She took me by the hand and dragged me to the back of the car. She opened the rear door, and that's when I saw why she needed my help. The entire back of her SUV was filled with bags from a bunch of different stores.

"What is all this?" I asked.

Sage reached in to grab a few bags and said, "I'll show you when we get inside. Can you grab the rest of the bags for me?"

I shook my head in amusement, laughing on the inside, and ordered, "Take what you have. I've got the rest."

"Okay."

Sage turned and walked away with her bags as I gathered up the rest of them. When I met her inside, I dumped the bags I'd brought in on the love seat where she had put the bags she brought in.

"Okay, sit down," she instructed.

Not wanting to do anything that would rile her up, I did as she asked.

Once I was seated on the opposite couch, Sage explained, "So, after I got through my bout of nausea earlier today, I started thinking. And I decided that I want to start a tradition."

"A tradition?" I repeated.

Sage grinned and nodded before she walked over to the bags. She started dumping them out all over the floor in the living room. I didn't know exactly what I was looking at, but I saw a lot of baby pumpkins, fall colors, cornucopias, turkeys of every shape and size, candles, and so much more.

After she'd emptied them all out on the floor, she knelt down beside everything and looked up at me. She beamed, "Big holidays."

"What?"

"Big holiday celebrations with decorations," she semi-repeated. "We're having a baby. We need to start our traditions."

I let out a laugh. "Sage, the baby isn't going to be here until next year," I reminded her.

"And?" she asked, her eyes narrowing at me.

Clearly, that wasn't the right thing to say. So, I quickly backpedaled. "And I think it's great that you're looking to figure it all out this year so that we get it all right for the baby's first year of holidays."

Her face lit up as she stood and walked over to me. "Really?" she asked as she settled herself in my lap. "You really mean that?"

I searched her face, trying to memorize the look on it, and assured her, "Yeah, babe. I really mean that. I'll help you with all the decorating, too."

She brought a hand up and cupped the side of my face. "You know you're responsible for this, right?" she asked.

My brows pulled together. "What do you mean?"

Sage took in a deep breath and blew it out before she explained, "When I was a little girl, my parents always made a big deal out of the holidays. They were always special and filled with so much fun and excitement. Even the ones that didn't have presents included. There was just something about each and every holiday that made it memorable. I knew I'd spend the few days before Thanksgiving helping my mom prepare the desserts or meals. I can even remember tearing up the bread for the stuffing. Christmas was all about the decorations, presents, songs, and movies. And baking cookies. Every holiday was magical."

She paused a moment, seeming to be struggling with something. I gave her a minute to collect herself and was happy to see that she did.

That's when I learned what was suddenly upsetting her. Because with her eyes staring off into the room, she continued, "But at some point, things changed. My parents are older now and they still do the holiday thing, but it's not like when I was little. I think it became something different for me over the last few years because with every year that went by, I felt like I wasn't going anywhere in my life. I had my friends and my job, but that was it. There was nothing new or exciting happening. I just wondered if I was ever going to have the chance to make memories with a family of my own. And since it wasn't happening, the holidays started feeling less and less special."

Sage turned her attention to me. "Then you walked into my life two months ago and revived me, handsome. I feel excitement again about the holidays, and I'm finally going to be able to create memories with you and our baby. I can't tell you how happy that makes me."

I hated knowing that Sage ever felt sad in her life, but it felt good to know that I'd been able to turn that around for her. I thought she should know just what she'd done for me, too.

So, I shared, "I have an idea of how it makes you feel, Sage."

Her features grew curious as she waited for an explanation.

"The guys I work with are some of my closest friends," I started. "Over the last few years, they've all met women with whom I know they're all going to be in it for the long haul. I was the last remaining single guy in the bunch. It was starting to sting. The day I saw you on the television, I'd just returned home from my buddy's party feeling the lousiest I could remember feeling in a really long time. I get what you're saying about feeling revived, babe. Because as soon as I saw you, my heart was pounding in my chest. I had this gut instinct that you were the woman I'd been waiting for all this time."

"You're going to make me cry," she warned me.

"Don't cry," I said softly before I touched my lips to hers. "As a kid, holidays weren't the same for me as they were for you. My mom did the best that she could, and I was always grateful. But I'm excited that I'll have the chance to give our baby everything I didn't have. And I know my mom is going to be overjoyed to have a grandchild to spoil, which kind of brings me to something I wanted to talk to you about."

Sage waited patiently for me to continue.

"I want to introduce you to my mom," I declared.

"Really?" she asked with a smile on her face.

I nodded.

"When?"

"Well, I know you have to work Wednesday and Thursday this week, and you're off this weekend," I began. "I was thinking you might want to catch up on some rest on Friday but that maybe we could go and see her on Saturday. It's up to you, though. I know she'll be open to anything."

Tipping her head to one shoulder, Sage asked, "Have you told her about me?"

"Yeah," I confirmed. "She doesn't know yet that we're living together or that we're expecting a child. I wanted us to be able to tell her that together but thought it was best to introduce the two of you first. She's really excited to meet you, and I promise you she's the sweetest woman you'll ever meet."

Sage's fingers ran through my hair as she replied, "I have no doubts about the kind of woman she is. Based on everything you've told me about her and the fact that I think she did a heck of a job raising a man like you, I'm pretty sure I'm going to like her. I'm okay with any day you want to do it."

Nodding, I confirmed, "I'll set it up then."

The next thing I knew, Sage was wrapping her arms around my body and cuddling into me. I held her close for a while, neither of us saying anything. This was what I'd been looking forward to all day today. Spending time with Sage, listening to her talk to me about whatever crazy thoughts she had in her mind.

After the silence had stretched between us for a bit, Sage broke it. "Gunner?" she called.

"Yeah?"

"I think I'd like to have Thanksgiving here," she said.

"Okay?" I replied, unsure what she meant by that.

"I want our families here with us. And I think I'd like us to tell them together about the baby," she clarified.

Sage and I had kept the news of her pregnancy to ourselves. I hadn't shared it with anyone, and despite how sick she'd been over the last couple of weeks, Sage managed to keep it from everyone at work. But if I was being honest, I couldn't wait to tell the world.

"That's completely fine with me," I assured her. "Are your parents coming out here?"

"They will if I ask them to," she answered.

"And you don't think you're going to feel too tired to cook?" I asked.

She laughed. "Probably. But I really want to do this. It's important to me, so I'll push through. Considering it worked out and I've got next Wednesday and Thursday off, I'll use part of the day Wednesday to prepare things. And maybe this Sunday, I'll run out to get the things I'll need."

"Levi's going to be closing the office next Wednesday through Friday, so I'll be here to help you with anything you need," I promised.

"I love you," she proclaimed.

After giving her a kiss on the cheek, I returned the same sentiment.

"We should start our decorating now if we're going to get everything done before next week," she advised.

"How about you let me feed you and that baby first?" I suggested. "Then, we can work on the decorations."

"Hmmm. What are you going to make me, handsome?"

"Do you want anything special?" I asked.

She shrugged. "Not really."

"Then, how about some rice, vegetables, and chicken?"

Sage grinned before she shared, "If I don't have to cook, I'm not complaining."

I let out a laugh. Things were so easy with her. I'd been

waiting before taking things to the next level between us until after we had a few disagreements and could work through them. But the way things were going, I wasn't sure we'd ever have any.

It was strange, too. Because I'd had my fair share of relationships over the years, and I often wondered what I'd been doing wrong that nothing ever seemed to last. It was easy back then to question myself and wonder if I was just being too picky. Because no matter how hard I might have tried with another woman, it never worked out. In those moments, it was difficult not to get down and blame myself for it all. But looking back on it now, I realized that I shouldn't have thought of it like that. There wasn't necessarily anything wrong with any of the women I dated. They just weren't the one for me.

Because none of them were Sage.

I kissed her again, pulled back, and instructed, "Call your parents and let them know you want them to come out here next week. I'll get dinner started."

"Okay," she agreed.

With that, as was always the case with us, we kissed each other again before separating ourselves from one another.

Then I got up to go make my woman some dinner while she called her parents. And for the first time in my life, I was beyond excited about the holidays. I couldn't wait to do all the things that Sage wanted that would allow the both of us to create memories that we'd hold close for the rest of our lives. Beyond that, I wanted to give those memories to our children.

Yes, children.

Because I had no doubts that Sage and I weren't going to stop at just one.

CHAPTER 9

Sage

For the last few weeks, I'd been making a valiant effort to focus on the good things surrounding me. Even when something challenging rose to the surface, somehow, I found a way to see the good in it.

My morning sickness was one great example of this. I had been really struggling with it, but once I took a step back and realized just how lucky I was to even be pregnant, it made it easier to cope. I also kept reminding myself that Dr. Perry had mentioned that the morning sickness was a sign of a healthy implantation and pregnancy. When I did, I considered the fact that I could have been dealing with complications and worrying about the health of my unborn baby.

I was essentially counting my blessings these days.

One of the biggest of those was Gunner.

I didn't know what my expectations were about what life would be like when I found a man that I could see myself with for the long haul, but I knew they didn't include what I had gotten. Of course, I had no doubts that I'd hoped for something and someone so wonderful, but I don't think I ever actually believed I'd get it.

Now, I considered myself to be extremely lucky.

Because Gunner was everything I could have dreamt of and more.

He was so attentive and incredibly helpful. And he loved me in a way I never even knew was possible. It was as though his days started and ended with me. I loved that because I felt the same way about him.

And while I knew it didn't matter what other people thought of what we had between us, I hoped they could see it. Those people being our parents. I wasn't necessarily concerned about my parents. Not only did they trust my judgment, but they'd also be around him for a few hours and fall in love with him. It wouldn't be for any reason other than seeing the way he treated me and how happy he made me.

I called them earlier in the week and told them I wanted them to come out to see me for Thanksgiving. Considering I moved back to Windsor at the end of July, and my parents hadn't been out to visit me yet, they jumped at the chance.

"I'm really excited about you guys coming out here, Mom," I started after she had accepted my invitation to visit.

"Me, too. We've missed you so much. I was really hoping we'd get to see you for the holidays, but I also knew that you needed time to settle in back in Windsor. I told your dad that if Thanksgiving went by without us seeing you, we'd have to figure out how to bring up the subject of a visit for Christmas," she returned.

"You're welcome to come and visit me anytime you want," I assured her.

She hesitated a moment before she replied, "I think we know that, but we don't want to step on your toes either."

I hated that she thought she'd be inconveniencing me by coming for a visit. I hoped that would all change once I was able to share the good news with her. It was important to me that my parents played a big role in my child's life.

"Well, I think it's important I tell you now that when you get here, I have someone I'd like you to meet," I informed her.

She gasped. "You've met someone?" she asked.

"Yeah," I swooned. "And he's an incredible man, Mom. He's really important to me."

"How long have you known him?" she wondered.

I let out a laugh. "We actually knew each other in high school. I used to have a crush on him back then, but he never asked me out. We reconnected about two months ago, though, and things are serious between us."

"Then I'm looking forward to meeting him," she said. "And I'm certain your dad will be, too."

"Gunner's excited to meet the both of you as well," I shared.

"Gunner?" she repeated.

"Yes. His name is Gunner Hayes."

"That's different," she declared.

I rolled my eyes. "It's not exactly like Sage is a name you hear every day either, Mom."

She laughed and explained, "I know. That's why I was thinking he sounds like the perfect guy for you. You both have unique names. It works."

Only my mom would think a lifelong partnership could be decided based on how the names of the individuals sounded together. It didn't bother me. In fact, if it helped her favor the relationship between Gunner and me, I wasn't going to tell her how crazy she was.

I chatted with her a little while longer before we disconnected. Gunner was happy to hear that my parents agreed to come out for the holiday. He had been itching to tell someone about the pregnancy, so this was going to be the perfect opportunity.

Over the days that followed the call to my parents, my excitement for the holiday season grew. As he promised he would, Gunner helped me out and we got our home decorated.

Yes.

Our home.

During the decorating process, I'd say little things that I wasn't sure if he'd pick up on. But then I'd look at his face and know he hadn't missed it. It was only a simple statement like, 'Oh, our living room looks fantastic now,' and his features changed in a way that indicated he'd understood exactly what I'd said.

I hoped he realized that this was his home. While I still paid the mortgage, Gunner contributed in other ways. He'd pay for groceries and help with household chores. I never had to touch the garbage, either.

Considering we were still new and the fact that Gunner still had his condo, I didn't think it was wise to merge our finances. Of course, that didn't mean that I didn't hope we'd get there one day soon.

Until we got there, I wanted Gunner to feel like my house was his house. So, I made every effort to declare it as such. He didn't comment one way or the other, but I knew he was hearing it. I loved having him there with me. I wanted him to stay. And once I had the baby, I had no doubt about the kind of father he was going to be. There was no way I'd want to separate Gunner from his child. Quite frankly, there was no way I'd want to separate him from me.

So, after a great week together, it was now Saturday. It was a big day for me, too.

Because today, I was meeting Gunner's mom.

We were currently in his truck on our way to her place.

Thankfully, Gunner managed to set it up so that we could have dinner with her. Since I didn't typically start feeling better until late afternoon, getting together for brunch or even lunch might have been an impossible feat. I still struggled at work to keep it together, but nobody noticed. I had a feeling that when I was the focus of attention meeting Gunner's mom, I wouldn't be able to hide the nausea so easily.

To top it off, I wasn't only meeting her, but I was also meeting her husband. Gunner assured me that I had nothing to worry about, convinced that they'd love me. I wasn't exactly worried about it either way. Of course, I wanted them to like me, but when it came down to it, the only one whose opinion of me really mattered was Gunner.

I suspected that if his mom raised him to be the man that he is, she would trust his judgment in choosing a partner. So, that was my way of trying to stay focused on the positive.

Despite my best efforts to remain calm, when Gunner pulled into the driveway, I had to admit I felt a little nervous. As if sensing my nerves, my man reached over, gave my hand a squeeze, and ordered, "Relax. I promise she's going to love you."

"I'm trying," I assured him.

With that, we got out of the truck and walked to the front door. No sooner did Gunner knock on the door when an older man answered.

"Hey, guys. Come on in," he greeted us.

Once we were inside, Gunner made introductions. "Simon, this is my girlfriend, Sage. Sage, this is my stepdad, Simon."

I dipped my chin and offered a smile. "It's so nice to meet you," I said.

"Likewise, darling."

"Gunner, sweetie, I'm sorry. My hands were covered in oil and seasoning for the vegetables," a woman chimed in.

I looked to the side to see who I knew had to be Gunner's mom walking toward us. Her son was the spitting image of her.

"It's okay, Ma," Gunner replied. "This is Sage, the woman I've been telling you all about. And Sage, babe, this is my mom, Catalina."

"I'm so excited to finally meet you," she declared as she moved forward to hug me. When her arms were wrapped around me, she instructed, "And you can call me Cat."

"It's nice to meet you, too," I said, hugging her back.

After we separated, she explained, "The veggies need another ten minutes, but I've got everything else nearly ready to go. If you want to come in, get something to drink, and make yourself comfortable, we'll be ready to eat shortly."

With that, Gunner put a hand to the small of my back and guided me farther into the house. His mom and Simon were ahead of us, and she was continuing to talk.

"I made sangria and pomegranate spritzers," she started. "But I also have wine and beer. Is there anything, in particular, you'd like?"

My eyes shot to Gunner's. We were planning to tell everyone about the pregnancy next week, so I didn't know what to do. The last thing I wanted to do was offend his mom.

Gunner was quick on his feet. "Sage isn't big on alcoholic drinks, Ma," he explained.

"Oh, well, that's okay. The pomegranate spritzers don't have any alcohol. I also have water and sweetened peach tea."

"The pomegranate spritzer sounds amazing," I said.

"Perfect. I'll get one of those for each of us. Gunner, you want a beer?"

"Yeah, that's fine," he answered.

"Simon, can you grab a beer for Gunner and yourself?" she asked.

Simon did as Cat asked and got beers for the boys while she got the drinks for us girls. While we waited for the vegetables to finish in the oven, Cat asked Gunner about work. He didn't provide her specific details about any cases he was working on, but he let her know that things had been relatively easy over the last few weeks. They hadn't had any major cases to deal with other than their routine work.

She seemed relieved by this news and went on to ask how all of his co-workers were doing. "Everyone is good. As you know, Cruz and Lexi got married at the beginning of September. They're in the honeymoon stage right now. Levi and Elle are adjusting well to parenthood. Trent and Delaney are expecting their first together. Holden and Leni are wedding planning. And I'm pretty sure Tyson's going to be proposing to Quinn soon. He hasn't said anything yet, but I have a good feeling about it," Gunner shared.

"That'll be exciting to have another wedding in the group," Cat returned. "What about Dom, Lorenzo, and Pierce? They're all doing well, too, right?"

Nodding, Gunner confirmed, "Yeah. Dom's busy with the twins but ready for more. Lorenzo is enjoying Jolie. They aren't rushing anything. And Pierce and Zara are busy spoiling Jax."

No sooner did he finish updating her on all the people he worked with that I had yet to meet, when her eyes came to mine. It seemed she was just about to say something when a timer started beeping.

Her shoulders fell and she turned toward the oven. From that point forward, we all spent the next few minutes carrying our drinks and the dishes filled with food into the dining room. When we were all seated and had filled our plates, the conversation turned from Gunner to me.

"So, Sage," Cat started. "While Gunner has told me that you're a meteorologist and how much he really likes you, he didn't give me a whole lot of details about how you two met."

I let out a laugh and shared, "Oddly enough, Gunner and I actually met each other back in high school."

Her eyes widened in shock. "Really?" she asked.

I nodded. "Yeah, but I ended up moving at the end of our junior year when my father's job transferred him to Oregon."

"When did you move back here?" Simon asked.

"At the end of July," I answered.

"And then they sent you out to deal with those hurricanes," Cat chimed in. I could tell from the tone of her voice she was upset about it.

Nodding, I explained, "Yeah, but it's part of the job. I don't typically mind it. In fact, I think it's exciting to go out and cover storms like that. But if I'm being honest, that was probably the scariest I've ever been involved in."

She shook her head in disbelief and amazement. Her eyes went to Gunner. She studied him a moment before she returned her gaze to mine. "He was a wreck after that second storm hit."

Instantly, I felt a burn hit the top of my chest.

"The more time that went by without word from you, the worse he got," she went on. "I don't think in all my years I've ever seen my son more scared than he was for those several days. Considering the things he can get involved in with work, that's saying something."

Gunner hadn't ever hidden his feelings about how scared he was after that storm hit. I knew he was deeply affected by it. But I never expected that he shared those feelings with anyone else. Having his mom tell me just how distraught Gunner was when he hadn't heard from me made it difficult to breathe.

I turned my head to the side and looked at Gunner. He noticed the change in my mindset and asserted, "But she's here now. She's safe. And all is good."

"I'll give you that," she said. "I talked to him the day after you got back, and he was like a completely different person. So, he's right. Everything is all good now."

I felt a bit of relief with that, and luckily, Simon changed topics. "Hey Gunner, after dinner I need your help with something in the garage. I've been working on restoring that '68 Fastback Mustang, and I need a second set of hands with something. It'll probably take about ten minutes if you wouldn't mind."

"Sure," Gunner agreed. "How's it coming along anyway?"

As Simon went on to tell him about the Mustang he was restoring, everything went back to normal for me. And from that point forward, the conversation was much lighter.

Following dinner, just as they had planned to do, Simon and Gunner went out into the garage. Before they went out, they had helped clean up the dinner dishes. So, Cat and I had gone to sit down in the living room.

"I hope you know it wasn't my intention to upset you earlier, Sage," she said.

"I know," I assured her. "It was… it was a really tough time for me, too. Gunner and I had only just reconnected the night before I had to leave, so it was really hard for the both of us. He already shared with me how worried he had been, so I knew before you even said anything about it. I think it's just that hearing it from someone else made me understand just how difficult it was for him. Even still, I think he might have downplayed how much it bothered him."

Cat laughed and admitted, "That doesn't surprise me. He's always been that way."

My brows pulled together. "In what way?" I wondered.

She took in a deep breath before she explained, "I don't know how much Gunner has shared with you about his childhood, but it wasn't easy for us."

"He didn't tell me all the details," I replied. "But he indicated that things were pretty tough for the two of you."

Cat nodded. "We were doing alright for quite a while. It wasn't exactly the easiest, but we were managing. Gunner didn't ask me for anything at all. One year, though, he expressed interest in snowboarding. I picked up an extra job to be able to pay for him to do it. And over the next couple of years, he worked hard and became one of the best in his age group."

I sat there utterly shocked. I had no idea Gunner had been into snowboarding. "Really?" I asked. "I don't remember that about him from high school. And not to give you too much information here, but I paid attention to him way back then."

"He quit before he got to high school," she mumbled.

"Why?"

She closed her eyes and took in another deep breath. I knew whatever she was about to tell me was going to be upsetting. "He was so good," she sighed. "Gunner worked so hard to be the best he could be at snowboarding. And it paid off. When he was just twelve years old, he took first place at a contest that had over fifty kids in his age group. I knew that he had the potential to go far with it. But just two weeks after that contest, I lost my full-time job. I picked up extra shifts at my part-time job and tried to find more work, but I didn't have any luck. I tried not to let Gunner know how dire our situation was becoming, but I know he figured it out. He'd stare at me at dinner, and I knew it was because he saw me eating less and less just to make sure he always had enough to grow."

"I'm so sorry, Cat," I lamented. "I can't imagine how difficult that must have been for you."

"It's okay, dear. We survived. But I think it was due largely in part to the fact that Gunner sensed something was wrong and decided to quit snowboarding. I hated that for him because I knew not only how much he loved it but also just how good he was. Unfortunately, our situation became so desperate that I couldn't insist he stick with it."

My heart hurt hearing this.

It also shed a lot of light on why Gunner was the way he was. It explained why he insisted on the two of us moving in together. Of course, he'd shared that he was raised by a single mom, but I hadn't realized just how bad their struggle was.

What I hated most of all was learning that Gunner had a dream. And he had to give up on that dream.

Right then and there, I made a promise to myself that no matter what happened between us down the road, I'd never stop Gunner from doing what he wanted to do to provide our child with the best opportunities to live out his or her dream. And I had no doubt that he had every intention of doing just that.

"This is so heartbreaking," I murmured.

"I'm sorry, Sage. I shouldn't be saying all of this to you and upsetting you. I know my son. He's going to walk in here, see you upset, and then never want to bring you back."

I didn't want that to happen, so I took in a deep breath and pulled myself together.

"We should talk about Thanksgiving then," I suggested.

"My parents are coming out next week and I'm going to be introducing them to Gunner. I'd love for you and Simon to join us on Thursday if you don't have any other plans."

Cat smiled at me and promised, "I wouldn't miss it for the world. We'll be there."

"Great."

With that, Cat and I once again managed to move away from the heavy stuff. She asked me a bit more about my job, and I talked to her about hers. Apparently, she'd gotten to a point where she had had enough with struggling. After securing a better job years ago, she tried saving a little bit of money from each paycheck. When she finally managed to save up enough, she went back to school. It took her some time to get through it all, but she ultimately ended up getting her master's degree and currently worked as an occupational therapist. I admired her tenacity.

By the time Gunner and Simon came back inside, they never knew that Cat and I had ourselves on the verge of tears. I planned to talk to Gunner about it all, but I didn't think now was the time.

Several hours after we had arrived, Gunner and I left.

And once we were back in the truck making our way down the driveway, I declared, "She's going to be so excited when they find out about this baby."

"I have no doubts about that," he returned.

"I think she'll be a good grandma."

Gunner stopped at the end of his mom's driveway and looked over at me. "I told you she'd like you," he pointed out. "And you're right. She will be a good grandma. Because I know you'll see to it that she has the chance to be one."

"I love you, handsome."

"Love you, too."

CHAPTER 10

Sage

I BOLTED UP OUT OF THE BED AND RAN INTO THE BATHROOM.

Seconds after I started heaving over the toilet, I felt Gunner's presence behind me. The next thing I knew, he was holding my hair away from my face.

I was struggling because even though I felt sick, I was trying to be quiet.

It was Thanksgiving Day.

And last night, my parents spent the night in my guest bedroom. It was at the opposite end of the hall, but I didn't want to risk them hearing me hurling either.

Gunner and I had planned to share the news with both sets of parents today at the same time. The last thing I wanted was for my parents to find out before Gunner's did.

"Shut the door," I requested, my voice strained.

Gunner managed to shift himself around my body and close the door without letting go of my hair. I couldn't pay much attention, but it was my guess that he must have kicked out his leg to shut it.

Convinced that there was enough of a barrier between where I was and where my parents were, I managed to handle business. When I finished, Gunner asked, "You okay?"

I gave him a nod and moved to the sink to brush my teeth.

And just like he'd been doing for me every day, Gunner walked out of our bedroom and went downstairs to get me something small to eat. It was still early, way too early to be up on a holiday, but if I didn't get something in my stomach, I'd end up getting sick again. I found that Dr. Perry had been right. Small, frequent snacks in between meals did the trick. As the day progressed and I got more food in my system, the unpleasant feeling went away.

After brushing my teeth, I made my way back out to the bedroom and climbed into bed. It was just before six-thirty. I didn't need to be up this early and knew I'd have a long busy day on my feet. I was going to take advantage of all the rest I could get.

This morning, I was feeling particularly tired. While it wasn't what I'd normally consider a late bedtime, I went to bed later than usual ever since I learned I was pregnant. My parents arrived early yesterday afternoon. After spending the better part of the day catching up with them, I got in my bed a good two hours after when I'd normally get in bed.

On the bright side, the meeting between Gunner and my parents had gone really well. As I had suspected, they liked him. No, that wasn't accurate. They loved him.

I could see it in the way my father spoke to him and the way my mother looked at him. And after they spent a good deal of time talking to him about what he does for a living and asking the both of us about how we met, things grew even more comfortable. My dad and Gunner ended up watching a football game on television while my mom and I worked on baking some desserts in the kitchen.

That's when I got more proof of how my parents felt about Gunner.

"You're in love," my mom announced, her voice soft.

I looked up from where I was working on my autumn spice cake and found my mom staring into the next room where Gunner and my dad were sitting. She was looking at the man who'd stolen my heart.

When she turned her attention to me, I confirmed, "Yes, I am."

Smiling at me, she shared, "I had a feeling that was the case when I spoke to you on the phone last week. I could hear it in your voice when you talked about him. But I can see it now in the way you look at him."

"He really is an incredible man, Mom," I started. "I've never known anyone like him."

"It's such a relief," she sighed.

"What is?" I asked.

She glanced in Gunner's direction a moment before she looked back at me and clarified, "To know that he feels precisely the same about you. I don't know. I know you've dated other people, but there's something different about Gunner. He looks at you like you're some lost treasure he's found. I like that. I like knowing my daughter has a man in her life who thinks that about her."

My mother's words warmed my heart. Not just because she knew how much Gunner and I felt for one another, but because she managed to see it in the very short time she'd been around the two of us together.

"It feels the same to me," I assured her. "It's like I've been searching forever to find him, and suddenly, he just appeared. Obviously, I told you that we knew each other in high school, but it was never more than just as friends. It's crazy to think that we both liked each other more than that back then, and neither one of us acted on it."

"I'm glad you guys didn't," she stated.

I shot her a questioning look. "Why?"

"Lots of reasons," she began. "But there are two big ones. First, I would have hated for you to find someone like him back then only to have to tear you two apart when Dad's job forced us to move to Oregon. The bigger reason, though, is that I'm not sure you would have gotten to this point if you'd have started something back then. You both were young. While I know it's not unheard of for two people who meet and date in high school to end up together, I don't think it would have worked out well for you guys. It's doubtful you two would have had the respect and appreciation for each other that you do now."

"You don't think so?"

She shook her head. "I didn't know him as a teenager, so I can't say. But I knew you. And while you were mature for your age, you were still a kid. It's tough for kids to make all the right decisions. There are a lot of adults who can't manage that. I think it's better that you were only friends then. It gave you both time to go through things in your life. Now, the two of you are at a place in each of your lives where you have experience. You know what you want in a relationship."

She had a point. Sometimes, I found myself wondering about what could have been if Gunner and I had started something all those years ago. And it's been easy to feel frustration over the fact that I missed out on all that time with him. But maybe my mom was right. We only had that lingering attraction between us. Acting on it too soon might have destroyed any chance we had in the future.

"I never really looked at it like that," I agreed with her. "When I first learned that he felt the same way about me that I did about him back then, I can admit I was a bit frustrated. But

I think you might be right. It's much better that we didn't act on anything until now."

With that, my mom gave me a smile and a nod of approval. Then, we got to work on finishing up our Thanksgiving desserts. Every so often, Gunner would walk out to grab a beer for my dad or himself. And when he did, he'd be certain to kiss me or even talk with my mom and me for a bit. I knew she saw that and loved it for me.

And now as I laid here in bed, I hoped both of my parents would continue to see the love Gunner and I had for one another and how solid we were after we shared the news of our pregnancy.

Just then, Gunner walked back into the bedroom carrying a glass of water and an apple-cinnamon muffin.

I smiled at him and sat up in the bed again. As I took the plate from him, I said, "Thank you. I wasn't expecting a muffin this morning."

He shrugged. "You made them fresh last night. I figured it was best for me to go down and get what was easiest so I didn't get stopped by anyone along the way. They might wonder why I'm bringing you breakfast in bed."

"I take it nobody was awake?"

"Not yet," he confirmed.

I lifted the muffin to my mouth and took a bite. It was good, and I thought Gunner deserved to be rewarded for his efforts this morning, so I held it out to him to take a bite.

He shook his head. "It's for you and the baby," he insisted.

"One bite isn't going to hurt," I noted. "Besides, I want to know if you like my baking."

As soon as I said that, Gunner opened his mouth and took a bite. After he chewed and swallowed, he assured me, "It's really good, but I already knew that."

"How?"

"I had one last night," he confessed.

My eyes widened. "You didn't."

He looked at me sheepishly. "Can you forgive me?" he asked.

"Only if you promise to stay in bed with me for a little longer. Yesterday wore me out. I'm exhausted."

Gunner leaned toward me, nuzzled his face into my neck, kissed me there, and said softly, "I think I can manage to stay in bed with you for a lot longer. Whatever you need, Sage."

I polished off the muffin in no time at all. When I finished, I gave him a kiss and thanked him again. Then, we cuddled up under the covers again. Within minutes, I was asleep.

"Simon, Cat, these are my parents, Mike and Rose. Mom, Dad, this is Cat and Simon."

Gunner and I took a step back while our parents exchanged greetings with one another. Gunner's parents had just arrived. It was approaching noon, but we hadn't planned on having lunch until closer to one-thirty.

This morning, Gunner and I ended up eating breakfast with my parents. I hadn't been feeling well, and I was terrified that my parents were going to notice. If they did, they didn't mention it. I think it might have helped that Gunner made a comment about feeling tired. I knew he wasn't actually tired, but I think he realized just how exhausted I was.

All morning I struggled with nausea. Even though I didn't expect I'd get sick, I ended up having a few moments when I'd excuse myself. I'd run upstairs to the bathroom or just to rest on my bed for a few minutes while the wave of nausea passed.

Originally, I thought we'd wait until later in the day, but I just couldn't. I didn't think I'd be able to last much longer without telling them. So, while they greeted one another, I looked up at Gunner and mouthed, 'I want to tell them now.'

He dipped his chin confirming his agreement.

We all managed to make our way out to the kitchen and I asked, "Cat, what can I get you to drink?"

"I made my cranberry champagne cocktail," my mom chimed in.

She did? When did she do that?

"Oh, that sounds wonderful," Cat marveled.

"It is," my mom assured her. "It's Sage's favorite."

Fuck.

Cat's brows pulled together as Simon asked, "But I thought you didn't like alcoholic drinks?"

Fuck.

"Who? Sage? Are you kidding? She can down several of those cocktails in no time at all," my dad assured him.

This couldn't seriously be happening right now. Gunner's mom and stepdad might have liked me before. Now, they were going to think I was a drunken liar.

"Oh," Simon returned, surprised. "She and Gunner were over a few days ago and he said that she—"

"I'm pregnant," I blurted, cutting him off.

All eyes came to me. Every single one of them had shock registered in them. Except for Gunner's. His eyes were twinkling. He couldn't have been happier. In fact, I noticed he was fighting a smile.

"What?" my mom asked.

"I'm pregnant," I repeated. "I'm not against alcoholic

beverages. I have enjoyed them on occasion, in fact. But Gunner and I wanted to wait until we were all together to share the news. We're expecting a baby. You're all going to be grandparents."

Silence had filled the room.

That silence felt like it had lasted an eternity, but it was mere fractions of a second later when my mom and Cat reacted. Cat's hands flew to the top of her head while my mom's palms were pressed together in front of her face.

"Are you serious?" Cat asked, the tears in her eyes.

Gunner had moved to stand next to me at this point. He confirmed, "Yes. Sage is going to be twelve weeks tomorrow, and the baby is due at the beginning of June."

Immediately, the mothers moved toward us and engulfed us in their arms.

"Oh, Sage," my mom cried softly in my ear. "I couldn't be happier right now. Congratulations."

"Thank you. It's been so hard not to just blurt it out, but we really wanted to tell all of you together."

"It's okay," she assured me before stepping back and framing my face in her hands. "My girl is going to be a mom."

I smiled at her as tears filled my eyes. Suddenly, I felt a hand at the middle of my back. My mom dropped her hands from my face and moved to congratulate Gunner. His mom stood in front of me, tears spilling down her cheeks, as she rasped, "Congratulations, Sage."

Then she pulled me into her arms. Between the pregnancy hormones and the emotions I felt telling our parents, I couldn't stop myself from letting my own tears fall. Cat held on tight, but eventually pulled back and allowed my father to pull me into his arms.

Once everyone had congratulated us, I looked at my parents and lamented, "I'm sorry that I kept running off this morning. I've been having such strong bouts of nausea in the earlier part of the day, and I just needed to run upstairs to lie down for a few minutes until it passed each time."

From that point forward, the moms insisted that I take it easy while they took over finishing up the Thanksgiving meal. Luckily, there wasn't a lot left to do since I'd managed to get some preparation done yesterday. As much as I didn't want to completely give up on it, I had been struggling and needed to at least accept some of their help.

The rest of the day was wonderful. Not only was everyone already in a festive mood because of the holiday, the unexpected news of a baby on the way left everyone feeling particularly overjoyed.

By the end of the night, though, I was wiped out. We'd had such a great day, and for the second night in a row, I hadn't gotten to bed anywhere near the usual time. I didn't mind, though, because it was the first family holiday gathering of what I hoped would be a new lifelong tradition.

And yes, I considered everyone to be family.

Because even though Gunner and I weren't married, we had made a baby. If that didn't qualify us as family, nothing would. Of course, that didn't mean that I wasn't hoping to one day get married to Gunner. In a perfect world, we'd get through these next few months, work together through what would probably be one of the most difficult and rewarding times of our lives, and really know for sure whether we were meant to be together.

There was no doubt in my mind that we'd be tied to one another through our child from here on out. I just hoped we wouldn't only be co-parents in our future.

The only way to hopefully avoid that was to nurture the relationship we had right now.

So, after Cat and Simon left, I declared, "I'm going to head up and take a shower. I'm wiped out."

"Okay," my mom replied. "I'm not going to be far behind you. Once I finish my tea, I'm heading to bed, too."

"Goodnight. I'll see you in the morning."

"Goodnight," my parents said in unison.

My eyes shifted to Gunner. He was looking over at me from his spot on the couch with a beer in his hand and a look of adoration on his face.

I suspected he was going to tell me that he planned to finish his beer and that he'd be up afterward, but he didn't say anything at all. Instead, he stood and moved toward me. He kissed my cheek before directing his attention to my parents. It was not surprising to see that they had watched everything he'd just done.

"Thanks for coming out here to celebrate the holiday with us," he started. "It means a lot that we could share this day with both sets of our parents."

My parents' faces warmed before my father responded, "Thank you for having us. This has been a Thanksgiving I know we won't ever forget."

With one arm wrapped around my shoulders, Gunner curled me into his body. "We'll see you in the morning. Have a good night," he told them.

Beaming up at us, my mom returned, "You too."

At that, Gunner and I turned to walk out of the room. As we climbed the stairs after he disposed of his beer bottle in the kitchen, I couldn't help but recall my father's words.

This was a Thanksgiving my parents didn't think they'd ever forget.

I felt the same way.

Because Gunner had come back into my life and given me more than I could have ever imagined. With it, he revived my love for the holidays and being with family. For that reason, despite how tired I was, I planned to show Gunner just how much I appreciated him.

CHAPTER 11

Sage

A DEEP, SEXY GROWL CAME FROM SOMEWHERE AT THE BACK OF Gunner's throat.

The sound made me feel powerful, so I pulled back, gave him a seductive look, and asked, "Do you like that, handsome?"

"I love it every time my little stranger comes out," he answered. "Especially when she's decided to initiate things like this."

My hand tightened around his cock and stroked along the length. Gunner's hand that had been resting on my ass pressed in just a bit harder.

He liked what I was doing.

I didn't know who I was trying to kid. *I* liked what I was doing.

It was the Monday following Thanksgiving and my first day off since the holiday. Today was also the first day I'd woken up and not needed to vomit. I had one or two waves of nausea, but it wasn't so bad that it sent me running to find the closest bathroom.

Gunner had gone in to work today, but came home early. Apparently, things had been relatively uneventful at work for him, so he decided to finish off his day from the comfort of our home.

We'd just had dinner and were in the middle of watching a movie. As I sat there next to him, I couldn't stop myself from staring. The longer I stared, the more turned on I became. I didn't know what it was for sure, but I had a feeling it was a combination of things that brought me to this point.

It was both physical and emotional. The physical part of it was the way he smelled, the way he looked, and the way his arms held my body close to his like I was someone he was trying to protect.

The emotional part was a bit more complicated. Simply put, I loved him. But it ran so much deeper than that. It was little things like cutting his day short at work to be home with me on my day off. It was the way he looked at me at any given time throughout the day. And then there was the determination he had in his eyes any time we talked about our baby.

Having learned a bit from him about his childhood combined with what his mom shared with me when I first met her, I had a feeling I knew where that determination stemmed from. Gunner wanted to be the best father he could. He wanted to be the father he didn't have. And I had no doubt he would make sure he did exactly that.

Our baby would be the luckiest child on the planet. Of that I was certain.

So, curled up next to him on the couch, feeling everything that I was, combined with pregnancy hormones, I pounced. In a good way.

I'd initially began stroking my hand over his thick, muscular, jean-clad thigh. Gunner's fingertips instinctively pressed into my side, curling my body farther into his, when my strokes led me higher up his leg.

Gunner made me feel good just by being him. I wanted to give him as much of that back as I could, even if he only felt just a fraction of it. So, I decided to unbutton his jeans and pull down the zipper.

"What are you doing, Sage?" he asked.

Tipping my head back, I smiled and explained, "Having a little fun."

Gunner cocked an eyebrow and repeated, "Having a little fun?"

My hand moved over the fabric of his boxer briefs that was covering his hard penis.

"I want to make you feel good," I started. "Isn't that okay?"

The corners of his mouth twitched. "It's okay," he confirmed.

Once I'd had his permission to continue, I curled my fingers around the waistband of his underwear and pulled them down, exposing him. I shifted my body so I was on my knees next to him, and Gunner helped me a bit as he lifted his hips a touch to push his clothes farther down his legs and out of my way.

With unhindered access, I wrapped my hand around the base of his cock and brought my lips to the tip. I swirled my tongue around the tip, listened to him groan, and began moving my mouth down his shaft. The sounds coming from him were more than I could have hoped for and made me never want to stop.

But I did.

Only because I wanted verbal confirmation that he liked what I was doing.

That's why I'd just asked him if he liked it.

And as he always did whenever he was surprised by

something I did, Gunner called me *his* stranger and assured me he loved it.

Loving that he was pleased with my performance thus far, I returned my attention to the task at hand and closed my mouth over him again. Gunner's hand tightened on my ass once more before he moved his fingers toward the edge of my panties. He slipped his fingers underneath my panties and immediately touched me right between my legs.

I don't know if he was surprised, but when he got there, it was clear to him that I was seriously turned on. Initially, he gently applied pressure and rubbed his fingers over me. But after he'd used my own wetness to lubricate the entire area, he drove two fingers inside.

I loved it, moaned to communicate that to him, and sucked him deeper into my mouth.

That earned me another groan from him. I loved that sound. I loved knowing I was making him feel that good.

Gunner wasn't slacking either. How he did the things he did with his fingers was beyond me. He knew precisely what to do to bring me right there… and then he'd stop. The first two times, I didn't mind. By the third, I couldn't take it anymore.

So, I took him as deep as I could in my mouth one last time and listened to him struggling to stay composed before I pulled back, straddled him, and pushed my panties to the side. Then I lowered myself down over him.

Gunner whipped my shirt over my head as I moaned at feeling so full with him inside me. Instantly, his face was in my chest, and he was kissing over the large swells of my breasts. My hips started moving slowly at first, but within moments, I had picked up my pace.

This man had done such a phenomenal job only minutes before that I was already so close. Part of the reason why I was moving so fast was that I was seeking to get that last little bit he wouldn't give me on his own. The other part of me was moving faster because this wasn't supposed to be about me.

This was about Gunner. I wanted to rock his world.

"Sage," he rasped, his tone indicating he was close to losing control.

"Gunner, baby, I love your cock," I panted. "I'm so close."

Gunner's eyes grew intense at my words. One of his hands went to my hip while the other reached up and landed behind my head. He tugged me forward, urging my mouth toward his. The moment our lips touched, sparks flew. Our orgasms hit simultaneously as we swallowed the sounds of each other's pleasure. They hit hard and long. It had to have been close to a minute later when I was still feeling tiny shudders consuming parts of my body.

My mouth disconnected from Gunner's, my forehead going to his shoulder. Our breathing was labored as we fought to regain our composure. It took some time, but I finally pulled myself together.

That's when I pulled back to look at Gunner.

His arms tightened around my waist and his features softened.

"You amaze me," he said gently.

Tipping my head to one side, I replied, "What?"

"Zero to one hundred in seconds," he started. "I thought we were just cuddling here to watch a movie. I didn't expect all the extras that I just got from you."

"Did you not enjoy it?" I asked.

A look of disbelief washed over him. "That's not a serious question," he deadpanned. "I'm not even going to respond to that."

"You brought it up," I defended myself.

"Sage, I brought it up because I love this side of you. I love how you can surprise me with these little things you do. That's all."

I swallowed hard and confessed, "I did it because you looked so handsome sitting here."

"That's all it took?" he wondered.

I shook my head. "It was a lot more than that," I admitted. "But that was a big part of it."

Gunner laughed and touched his lips to mine. "We should go get cleaned up," he suggested.

"Okay," I agreed.

At that, Gunner stood and ordered, "Wrap your legs around me."

So, I did.

Then he carried me upstairs so we could get cleaned up.

"Do you have a preference for a boy versus a girl?" I asked.

"For our baby?" Gunner asked.

We had just cleaned up and gotten ourselves in bed. I was on my side, Gunner was behind me with his arm draped over my hip. His hand was resting protectively on my belly.

"Yes. I was wondering if you'd given any thought to the sex of the baby and if you were hoping for one over the other," I clarified.

"I'm curious to know what we're having, but it honestly does not matter to me if I have a son or daughter. I know I'm going to eventually want both, so either one will be perfect."

I liked that. No, I loved it. Knowing that Gunner would

be happy regardless of whether we had a boy or girl made me love him that much more.

"What about you?" he asked. "What do you want?"

"A healthy baby," I immediately replied. "As long as he or she is healthy, I'll be happy."

Gunner shifted his body closer to mine, even though I could already feel it running the length of me. Somehow, he was successful in making me feel even more of him behind me.

When too much time had passed without a response from him, I decided it was the perfect time to talk to him about something that had been on my mind for days.

"Regardless of what we end up with—son or daughter—I want you to teach him or her everything you know," I shared.

"I'm going to do my best to always be a good example for our child," he assured me.

"I know that, Gunner. That's not what I'm referring to, though."

"What do you mean?" he wondered.

I took in a deep breath and blew it out before I said, "I want you to teach our children how to snowboard."

Gunner's frame instantly went solid behind him as his fingertips pressed into my abdomen. "What?" he asked, clearly shocked that I knew about his childhood.

"When we went over to your mom's house, she told me that you used to be a snowboarder," I started. "All these years, I never knew that about you."

"Yeah, I did it for a few years when I was a kid," he confirmed.

I brought my left hand down to my abdomen and rested my fingers on top of his hand. Then, I confessed, "Your mom told me that you were really good, but you gave it up because you knew how much the two of you were struggling."

Gunner didn't respond. I could still feel the tension running through his body. It bothered me to think that I'd brought up something that was painful for him.

As much as I didn't like that he was feeling this way, I realized it for the opportunity that it was. Over the last two-and-a-half months, Gunner and I really hadn't had any arguments. For the most part, we got along great. There were a few occasions when we had a difference of opinion, but we seemed to be able to easily talk through them. And it wasn't ever about anything truly important.

Maybe my mother was right. Gunner and I getting together now gave us a much better shot at having a long-lasting relationship. If we'd gotten together as teenagers, we might not have been so lucky.

"Gunner, talk to me," I urged him.

He hesitated a moment before he admitted, "I didn't think she knew the real reason why I quit."

"She's your mom," I noted.

"Yeah, but she had so much on her plate already," he reasoned. "I just assumed she bought my excuse of it being something I was no longer interested in."

"Would you?" I asked.

"Would I what?"

I dropped my shoulder back into his chest. Gunner shifted his body to give me enough room to fall to my back. It was dark in the room, but I could just barely make out his features. With his hand still resting on my abdomen, I covered it with my right hand and squeezed.

"If our baby decides one day to just up and quit something he or she is really good at and enjoys, would you accept an excuse that you knew couldn't possibly be the truth?"

Gunner's silence told me everything I needed to know. He wouldn't accept it.

"You gave up on your dream," I said softly. "I can't imagine how awful that was for you to have to endure."

His voice was husky when he replied, "It was better than the alternative. Either I could have been selfish and watch my mom starve because of it, or I could quit. There really wasn't a question in my mind about what to do. I loved snowboarding, but I loved my mom more. She was all I had."

I brought my hand up to touch his cheek. "I'm sorry that you were ever in a position where you had to make that choice," I lamented.

"I appreciate that, but I don't regret my decision."

I couldn't help but smile. "I know that, handsome. I just wish it wasn't one you had to make."

After that, the silence stretched between the two of us. It wasn't because we'd fallen asleep either. I started to wonder if maybe it had been a mistake to bring up the conversation with Gunner. Just as I was about to speak, he had already started.

"I promise I'll teach our babies how to snowboard," he said quietly.

Rolling toward him so that my front was pressed to his, I asked, "Babies?"

Gunner kissed my forehead before he replied, "You said it first."

"What?" I asked.

"You said you wanted me to teach *our children* how to snowboard," he reminded me.

As soon as he got the words out, I realized that was precisely what I had said. Our children.

"Do you want more than one baby with me, Gunner?"

"I've always wanted more than one child," he started.

"But before you came back into my life, I started wondering if it was ever going to happen for me. Honestly, when I walked into my place that night following Tyson's party, I was feeling the lowest I had in a long time. At that point, I was just thinking that I'd be happy to find someone with which to spend my life. The fact that I've not only got you now but also that we have a baby on the way already is more than I could have hoped for this soon."

I closed my eyes and squeezed my arm that was draped over his side. My hand pressed into the middle of his back as I kissed his chest.

"I love you," I whispered.

His voice was just as soft when he responded, "I love you, too."

Gunner made me feel safe and secure all the time. I believed that was just who he was. But there was this small part of me that was worried. Unfortunately, I couldn't hide that feeling and shared, "I really hope it's always this good."

"You hope what's this good?" he asked.

"This. What we have between us," I clarified. "In the last couple of years, I started feeling a lot like you had been feeling. No matter how happy I was with everything else in my life, this part of it really started taking its toll on me. I was feeling empty inside. It wasn't that I felt pressured by anyone or anything like that. It's just that I wanted this. I wanted exactly what we have right now. And now that we have it, I feel full inside. I feel revived. I'm just worried that as time passes, things might change."

Gunner brought his hand to my hip and gave me a squeeze. "Sage, babe, they're going to change," he started, his voice laced with strength and conviction. "We're having a baby. It's going to be tough to avoid any change. But I don't think that's a bad thing. Yeah, this might be new between us, but I know I love what we've started. From a very young age, I knew what kind of man I wanted to be. I'm telling you right now… you don't have anything to worry about."

I could have questioned him and asked how he was so confident, but I didn't. I had to have faith in him. I had to have faith in us. Clearly, Gunner wasn't concerned, and he had just as much reason as I did. If he believed in himself, in me, and in us, I figured that was the better place to be.

So, I accepted his words and said, "Okay."

Moments after I did that, I thought back to my conversation with my mom a few days ago. I started to think that maybe she wasn't completely right in her assessment. Gunner said it himself. He knew what kind of man he wanted to be.

As I laid there in his arms, I wondered how different things would have been if we'd acted on our feelings all those years ago. Just before I fell asleep, I concluded that Gunner was the kind of man who wouldn't have allowed it to be anything but what we had right now.

CHAPTER 12

Gunner

"We've got news," I declared.

Sage and I were sitting at a table with my co-workers, Tyson and Holden. Tyson's girlfriend, Quinn, and Holden's fiancée, Leni, were there as well.

It was roughly two weeks before Christmas and the six of us had decided to go out and get in the holiday spirit. Or, at least, that's how the women had put it.

Sage had met Tyson and Quinn a few weeks ago when I'd taken her out for lunch one afternoon. Tyson and Quinn were grabbing some food to go because they were going to be babysitting some of his nieces and nephews. After I introduced Sage to my friends, the women had hit it off and exchanged numbers.

Now, we were here because they'd kept in contact with one another and set it all up. Quinn, who had met Leni months ago, brought her into the fold, which is why Holden and Leni were here as well.

The women had conspired behind our backs and decided that we needed to get together for dinner, shopping, and Christmas festivities. I wasn't quite sure what the last part of that entailed, but I honestly didn't care.

Since she'd moved back here from Oregon, Sage hadn't really made a lot of new friends outside of work. Given the fact that we were together now, we were having a baby, and she wasn't going to be leaving Windsor, I thought it was a good idea for her to start forging friendships. Quinn and Leni were sweet women, and I knew they'd be great people for Sage to have in her corner.

For those reasons, I didn't put up a fight when Sage told me the plans for this evening. She was not only excited but also determined to create new traditions for the holidays. I wanted her to be happy, so if this was going to make that possible, I was all for it.

But before we came out tonight, Sage and I had decided that we wanted to share the news of her pregnancy with our friends. She was leaving it up to me to decide when the right time to share would be.

We'd all just finished our dinner, and I thought now was as good a time as any.

"We?" Quinn asked. "What news do *we* have?"

She was asking a question, but it was clear she already had an idea in her head as to what the answer might be.

I reached my hand out and held Sage's. After giving her a squeeze there, I smiled and said, "Sage is pregnant. We're having a baby."

Tyson and Holden looked utterly shocked. Quinn and Leni were positively beaming at the news.

"Wow! That's so exciting. Congratulations!" Leni declared.

"When are you due?" Quinn asked.

"June twelfth is the due date," Sage answered. "I'm fourteen weeks now."

"Congratulations," Holden said.

That was followed by more congratulatory words from the rest of the table. We all sat for a little while longer as the women discussed more details of the pregnancy.

A little while later, we ended up in a Christmas shop in downtown Windsor. Sage, Quinn, and Leni quickly moved deep into the store searching for ornaments, decorations, and gifts. The guys and I stayed close enough but didn't really get into the whole shopping thing.

That's when Tyson said, "A baby?"

I looked over at him, smiled, and nodded my head.

"Fourteen weeks already. That tells me she was pregnant when you were glued to that television in the office watching the reports on those hurricanes," he pointed out.

"Yeah," I confirmed his suspicions. "Obviously, it wasn't planned."

"Are you okay with it?" Holden asked. "It's kind of fast, isn't it?"

I shrugged. "Maybe. But it's Sage. I've known her since high school. Yeah, we never got together back then, but it's her. There's never been anybody like her. And I'm completely okay with the pregnancy."

"What about her?" Tyson asked.

"What do you mean?" I retorted.

"It's not just fast for you; it's fast for her. Did she handle the news okay?"

Before I had the chance to answer, Sage came bounding toward me. Quinn and Leni were still somewhere at the back of the store, out of sight. "What do you think about this?" she asked, holding a stuffed family of snowmen out to me.

Actually, that wasn't correct. It was snow people. A snow family, to be exact. A dad, a mom, and a baby.

"What about it?" I returned.

"I'm thinking of doing a snowman-theme for our holiday décor. Everything from ornaments for the tree and decorative pieces like this to dinnerware and serving platters. All of it can have snowmen on it," she explained.

It really didn't matter to me. "Babe, if that's what you want in the house, just get it. It really doesn't matter to me," I assured her.

"Are you sure? If you want something else, I'm happy to keep looking," she offered.

"Sage, I'm positive. Get whatever you want," I urged her.

Satisfied with my response and confident that I truly did not have an issue with whatever she decided to get, Sage smiled at me before she walked off toward the back of the store again.

I couldn't help but laugh as I felt Tyson and Holden's eyes on me.

"It seems Sage is handling the pregnancy news just fine," Holden surmised.

"You've got that right," Tyson agreed.

I shook my head, grinning. "She is now, but she wasn't in the beginning. She was worried that I was going to leave her to raise our baby on her own. The thing is, she wasn't concerned about being able to take care of the baby on her own. She just didn't want the pregnancy to end things between us."

"Well, you've clearly convinced her that you're not going anywhere," Tyson noted.

I nodded. "Yep."

"So, what's next?" Holden asked. "Are you planning to get married?"

Married.

I couldn't say the thought hadn't crossed my mind. It had. Many times. Ever since she was out on the work trip to North Carolina.

"We haven't talked about it," I admitted.

"Really?" Tyson asked.

Nodding, I told them, "I want to marry her; I know she's the one for me. But I've been a bit torn about bringing up the whole marriage thing with her."

"Why?" Holden questioned me.

I looked away from my friends and across the shop. Sage, Quinn, and Leni had all moved from the very back of the store to a spot where they were at least visible. We weren't close enough where they'd be able to hear anything we were talking about, though.

For a few moments, I watched as Sage excitedly chatted with her friends as they all picked up a million different things, eyed them, and put them back. Sometimes, if they found something they really liked, they'd hold on to it. At one point, Quinn had picked up an item and showed it to Sage and Leni. She said something to them and they all burst out laughing.

That's when I confessed, "I want that for the rest of my life, and I don't want to do anything to jeopardize it."

"Wouldn't asking her to marry you help you solidify things between the two of you and give you the reassurance that you'll have that for the rest of your life?" Holden pointed out.

"Of course. I just don't want her to think that I'm asking her to marry me simply because she's pregnant," I explained.

"You should talk to her about it," Tyson suggested.

"Don't wait for foolish reasons," Holden warned. "I did that, and it almost cost me the best thing that ever happened to me. You know what you feel, and I'm sure you're doing everything you've got to do to make sure she knows exactly what those feelings are."

That was the truth.

It might have been easy to look at our situation and assume that I was simply catering to Sage just because she was pregnant. But that wasn't it. I legitimately wanted to give her everything her heart desired. So, I often found myself agreeing with whatever she wanted. The extent of our disagreements was in inconsequential things, like differences in food or movie preferences.

"I'm planning to bring it up," I began. "I'm just waiting for the right time. I'll do it before the baby is born, though. I just thought it might be a good idea with her having to adjust to so much new stuff right now to hold back for a little bit longer. Besides, I promised her before I moved in that I wouldn't pressure her for anything else other than living together while she was pregnant."

"Talking to her isn't pressuring her," Tyson insisted. "And you never know… she might be over there right now stealing glances at you wondering why you haven't mentioned it."

My eyes shot in Sage's direction.

Sure enough, she was looking at me.

When our eyes locked, something changed in her features. She immediately grinned at me and waved.

I did the only thing I could do and let out a laugh.

But I did it thinking that my friends were right. Talking wasn't pressuring. And I needed to find a way to open up the lines of communication in a way that Sage wouldn't feel like that's where it was leading.

Sage

"What did he say about the snowmen?" Quinn asked.

I looked up from the tree adorned with more ornaments than I had ever seen on a Christmas tree and turned in the direction of my two newest friends, Quinn and Leni.

Aside from my co-workers, Quinn and Leni were the first two women I'd become friends with after moving back to Wyoming from Oregon. I couldn't have asked for a better pair.

I shrugged. "He doesn't seem to have much of an opinion beyond agreeing to whatever I want."

"That's not really a bad problem to have," Leni noted.

I grinned. "I know. But I feel like I'm waiting for the other shoe to drop," I shared.

"What? Why?"

Looking back in the direction of where Gunner was standing with Tyson and Holden, I couldn't stop myself from smiling. When I returned my attention to the girls, I admitted, "I feel so lucky to have him. He's honestly the perfect man."

"And this is a bad thing?" Quinn asked dubiously.

I shook my head and put the ornament I had been holding back on the tree. "Of course not. I love it. I love him. It's just… can this be real?"

Quinn tipped her head to the side, smiled, and pointed out, "The baby in your belly makes it very real, Sage. But beyond that, I can promise you that you're worried about nothing."

"How do you know?"

That's when Leni chimed in. "He looks at you the way Tyson looks at Quinn or the way Holden looks at me."

I swallowed hard. Even though I'd seen the way Tyson

and Holden looked at Quinn and Leni, I still asked, "What look is that?"

"The one that tells the whole world he can't believe that you're all his," she replied. "And how he struggles to comprehend how he ever lived without you. Trust us… Gunner is thanking his lucky stars that you're in his life the way you are right now."

Wow.

That was nice to hear.

It wasn't that I doubted Gunner or his intentions. I truly believed he was happy being with me. It was just that despite our talk a few weeks ago and Gunner's reassurance that there was nothing to be concerned about, I still found myself thinking the worst at times.

"It just seems impossible that I'm this lucky," I murmured as I picked up another snowman ornament. This one had four snowman heads stacked on one another. They were wearing red hats and none of the heads were stacked directly in the middle of the one beneath it. They were off to the side and resting at an angle. Each one had a different expression on its face, and I immediately decided I liked it. I pulled off a few more and put them in the shopping bag I'd gotten when I entered the store. Then, I continued, "It feels like the moment he showed up outside my news station is when my life started. Is that weird that I feel that way after only a short time? Somehow, it was like I was just going through the motions up until that point. Then he came along and revived me. It feels so good."

"It's not about luck," Quinn insisted. "Coming from me, that should mean a lot. We haven't really had a chance to sit down so I could tell you my whole story, but I'll do it one day. Just believe me when I tell you that this is what you were meant to have in your life."

"Don't question it," Leni urged me. "That's one thing I've learned in my life. I wouldn't be here doing what I do with the man of my dreams if I'd listened to my mind. I started following my heart a long time ago, and it's never led me astray. I can't stress it enough, Sage. Go with whatever your heart is telling you and everything will fall into place."

They were right.

I needed to stop allowing the thoughts in my head to get me to a point where I started questioning everything.

Gunner and I were doing this. We were together, and we were happy. I made a promise a couple weeks ago to have faith in us. I needed to stick to that.

"You're both right," I said. "I need to just allow myself to enjoy the positive stuff and forget about the unknown that's causing me stress."

Leni lifted an adorable snowman snow globe and held it out to me. "This is so cute," she said.

I took it from her, fell in love, and added it to my bag.

"So, how have you been feeling on the pregnancy front?" Quinn asked.

"I've actually been doing much better this last week," I started. "From the day I realized I was pregnant up until about a week ago, I had been struggling with morning sickness."

"That doesn't sound like fun," Leni stated.

Shaking my head, I confirmed, "It's been awful. But the doctor said that the sickness is a good sign of a healthy pregnancy. I tried to keep that in mind. Luckily, the nausea has now subsided, and I feel like I've got a lot more energy than I did weeks ago."

The girls and I continued to move through the shop, picking up items, and either added them to our bags or put them back. It wasn't long before my bag was near to overflowing. At that point, we had made it back toward the front of the shop where the guys were waiting for us.

The moment Gunner saw my overloaded bag, he came over, took it from me, and held it. "You should have told me you were planning to buy half the store, Sage," he ordered.

My eyes shot to his. "Why? Do you think it's too much?" I asked.

"Babe, I don't care what you get, but I don't want you lugging it all around," he clarified. "I would have come over sooner if I had realized how heavy this thing was."

I shrugged. "It really wasn't that bad," I assured him. "I was fine."

"Word to the wise," Tyson interrupted, his attention on Gunner. "Don't ever tell a pregnant woman she is incapable of doing something. I did that once with my sister-in-law and nearly had my head chopped off. Do what you can to minimize her load, but don't give her shit about it. You'll be saving yourself a ton of trouble."

Gunner let out a chuckle and responded, "So noted."

"I think I'm ready to head to the register to pay for this anyway," I told Gunner.

He dipped his chin and turned to start walking in that direction.

Before I could follow behind him, Quinn got close and whispered, "You made a good choice."

"On Gunner?" I asked.

She nodded. "Yeah. No doubt about it. But it's good you picked the snowmen, too."

I shot her a questioning look.

Seeing it, she didn't hesitate to explain, "Snowmen are perfect. If one pisses you off, you let him melt and you move on to the next."

At that, I burst out laughing.

When I pulled myself together, I saw Gunner looking at me in a way that told the world he couldn't believe that I was all his.

That look was all I needed to know that despite how funny and accurate Quinn's statement about snowmen was, I didn't think I'd ever need a new one.

Because the guy I had already wasn't going to do anything to intentionally piss me off to the point I'd want him to melt.

On that thought, I grinned at him before I walked over and met him at the register.

Needless to say, Gunner ended up buying all of our decorations.

CHAPTER 13

Sage

"THIS HAS BEEN THE BEST OF IT ALL."

That came from me.

I was curled up on the couch with Gunner. He had his legs stretched out in front of him, his ankles crossed with his feet resting on the edge of the coffee table. My head was in his lap; my body running the length of the couch. It was late in the evening on New Year's Eve, and the two of us were alone for what felt like the first time in a long time.

"What has?" he asked.

"Tonight," I answered. "I've thoroughly enjoyed the holidays, but there's just been so much going on for the last few weeks. Now, it's just the two of us, here on the couch, waiting to start a brand new year. I'm really loving this mellow mood after all the craziness of the past couple of weeks."

That was the truth.

We were approaching the end of the busy holiday season, and I have truly loved nearly every single part of it. First and foremost, these were my first holidays spent with Gunner. That alone would have been enough to make my year. Add in the fact that we were spending them together knowing that at this time next year we'd have a baby with us made our holidays even more special.

Beyond Gunner and our baby, I had truly had such an amazing couple of weeks. There had been so much fun with family and friends. It was great having the opportunity to enjoy being with people who meant the most to us. We all had limits, though.

And I was convinced I'd reached mine on several fronts.

When I made the move earlier in the year from Oregon back to Wyoming, I never imagined that I'd be in a serious, committed relationship with a man I loved and pregnant with his baby by the end of the year. But here I was.

We'd started a lot of new traditions this year, and I looked forward to adding new ones as the years went by. Yet, as much as I loved all of the wonderful things I'd experienced over the holidays, there wasn't a whole lot of downtime for Gunner and me. It seemed there was a constant stream of people around us. While I adored the people we had in our lives, I found that I had been craving time alone with just Gunner. Thankfully, I was now getting precisely that.

"Yeah, it's been a good time," Gunner agreed. "I'm excited about next year, too."

I let out a laugh. "Sometimes I think I've had too good of a time," I speculated.

"Is that even possible?" Gunner asked.

Twisting my neck in the opposite direction, my gaze shifted from the television to him. Gunner's eyes met mine. That's when I muttered, "If my pants are any indication, it is."

He looked confused. "What?"

"I can't fit in my jeans that well anymore," I shared. "If I struggle, I can get them on. But it's so uncomfortable."

Gunner's features softened. "You look amazing," he assured me.

"You have to say that," I noted. "If you didn't, you'd be setting yourself up for some serious trouble."

He chuckled and admitted, "I can't say you're wrong about that. I know I would be. But I'm serious, Sage. I think you look beautiful."

"It hurts," I told him.

Instantly, I felt his body tense underneath me. "What does?"

I wasn't sure where to start with the answer to that question. "My body," I finally said, believing that was the most accurate answer. "Especially my hips."

"Your body is making room for a baby, honey. I think that's supposed to happen," he offered gently.

I knew that. I expected it. In fact, I'd made it to the end of the first trimester and had gained a total of five pounds. Dr. Perry was happy with that, considering how sick I'd been throughout those first couple months.

"Dr. Perry might be happy with the weight I gained in the first trimester, but it's taking some getting used to," I started. "I've always been the same size my entire adult life, so I'm feeling the weight. I know it's all for the best. It's just an adjustment, that's all."

"That's even more of a thing to consider," Gunner began. "If Dr. Perry is happy with your weight gain, you keep doing what you're doing."

I shot him a look of uncertainty. "He might not like my weight gain now, though. I feel like I've put on a bunch of unnecessary weight over the holidays. That's kind of the reason I'm excited now. We're going to be getting back to our normal routines, which will allow me to be able to keep myself in check."

Gunner's hand came down and settled on my slightly rounded abdomen. "You're crazy if you think you are anything but beautiful at this very moment. I understand you might be struggling to adjust to the physical changes, but I want you to know how much I love your body right now. All the changes are driving me insane… in a good way."

I smiled softly at him.

He gently rubbed his hand over my belly as he continued, "Seeing this little bump, knowing you've got our baby growing inside you, sends me over the edge. It's the biggest turn on."

My eyebrows shot up. "Really?" I asked.

Gunner nodded. "No joke," he insisted. "Sometimes when I watch you on television, I can't stop myself from getting hard knowing what you look like with nothing on. Then I sit here feeling like it's taking forever for you to get home to me."

I had no idea he watched me on television. That was the first shock. But then to learn that he got turned on as I gave my weather reports was something else entirely. I wondered if I'd be able to go to work now without thinking about the fact that my baby's daddy was home watching me and getting excited for when I'd return.

Apparently, I'd taken too long to consider this because Gunner went on, "Sage, I need to know that you're not going to deprive yourself of food because you're worried about weight gain. Five pounds or fifty, it doesn't matter. What's important is that you're both healthy."

Instantly, I tried to calm his fears. "Gunner, I would never deprive myself and jeopardize our baby. I was merely pointing out the fact that I'm glad the holidays are nearly over. I won't need to worry about there being a never-ending supply of cookies and baked goods everywhere I turn. That's all. I mean, sure, I'm here complaining about aches and pains, but isn't that part of the whole process? The truth is, when I really take the time to think about what my body is doing, preparing for this baby, I can't help but love it all. I'll continue to nurture and enjoy the process. I promise you."

Gunner smiled and gave me a nod of understanding.

Suddenly, an idea hit me.

Gunner noticed and immediately asked, "What's that look for?"

I shot him a sneaky look and taunted him. "Well, I was just thinking that with this new information you gave me about watching me on television, I might have to do a little teasing."

"Teasing?" he asked, cocking an eyebrow.

"If you really love the changes in my body and you're getting excited seeing me when I'm wearing looser tops or jackets over my dresses just to hide any possibility that someone at work would find out before I was ready to tell them, I'm thinking it could be fun to let you see those curves now."

"And how do you plan to accomplish that?" he questioned me.

I grinned. "By wearing clothes that would accentuate the curves you're loving so much," I shared.

Initially, I hadn't been worried about the clothes I wore to work because I wasn't showing. My biggest worry was whether my co-workers would figure it all out based on the fact that I was so sick and exhausted those first few weeks. As I got better at concealing that, I started noticing small changes in my body. I didn't want anyone knowing until I was ready to share, so I started slowly making adjustments to my wardrobe. For the last several weeks, even after I'd shared the news at work, I thought I'd continue to wear things that hid my pregnancy from the camera.

But now I was reconsidering that decision.

Because I didn't need to hide it. There was nothing to be ashamed of, and my guy clearly liked it.

"I'll be ready for you every evening when you get home," he promised.

That would be the perfect way to end each work shift, so I wasn't going to complain. For the next little while, Gunner and I stayed there flipping back and forth between two different New Year's Eve television programs. Occasionally, we'd talk about the performances on one or the news on the other, but we mostly just enjoyed the silent comfort of one another's presence. I think it was just what we both needed after all of the festivities.

As exhausted as I'd been over the last few weeks, I thought it was a wise idea to take a nap earlier in the day today. It was important to me to be awake with Gunner when the clock struck midnight.

Before I knew it, there were only ten minutes left before it happened.

I turned away from the television again and looked up at Gunner. "It's almost the end of the best year of my life," I said softly.

With one hand still resting on my belly, Gunner brought the other to the top of my head. He ran his fingers through my hair as he simply searched my face for a few moments.

"It's not the best year of your life, Sage," he eventually replied.

I was a little shocked at his response. "It is," I insisted.

"I won't deny that this was an amazing year because that's precisely what it has been. But I promise you, babe, the best year of your life is yet to come."

Gunner spoke with such conviction it was hard not to believe him.

"How can you make such a promise?" I asked.

The minute the words were out of my mouth, something changed in Gunner's face. Seeing it, I knew it needed to brace myself. Because whatever he had to say was going to be big.

Gunner

Could I tell Sage everything I had planned for her over the next year?

I wanted nothing more than to spill my guts and share it all with her, but I worried she might think it was too soon. In any other situation, I would have had no problems sharing it with her. The pregnancy changed things for me, though. The last thing I wanted was to cause any sort of stress in Sage's life. The only thing that mattered to me right now was that she stayed happy so that she and our baby would remain healthy.

Things between us had already moved so quickly. I wasn't looking to pile more unexpected stuff on top of Sage for my own benefit and selfish needs.

That's what it felt like to me.

Selfishness.

More than anything else, I wanted to get down on one knee right now and propose to her. I wanted Sage for the rest of my life. I didn't have concerns about her not wanting to be with me, but I still wanted to make it official. Part of me thought that I should just do it. We were expecting a baby, and I wanted to do the right thing. I loved her more than I could ever fully express. So, it just seemed like the thing I needed to do. But the other part of me hesitated not only because of my concerns about causing her additional stress but also because I didn't want her to think I was only trying to do right by her.

All of this back and forth ultimately meant that I just felt stuck.

Still, as Sage looked up at me from where her head was resting in my lap, I knew I had to give her an honest answer to her question.

How can you make such a promise?

Her question flitted through my mind again.

"Because I love you," I finally answered. "What kind of man would I be if I didn't do what I could to make every day that goes by the best of your life?"

Sage's lips parted as she took in my words.

I managed to not get distracted by that look and continued, "We've had a lot happen in the last few months. Things have moved quickly. So, while I've got a lot of plans for us moving forward, I'm just giving us both some time to settle into what we have here. If I didn't think it would be too much too fast, I could have very easily taken this year up another notch."

Sage looked toward the television for a brief second before she looked back at me and dared, "You've still got two-and-a-half minutes left in this year to make it even more memorable."

Wanting to do just that for her, I slipped my hand under the back of her head and lifted her up. When we were face-to-face, our noses touching, I assured her, "I'm still planning to make next year the best of your life, Sage. But I'll do what I can to make sure you go out of this one with a bang."

"Sounds like a plan, handsome."

With that, I touched my lips to hers and kissed her. I continued to do that for the next two minutes and beyond. Suffice it to say that Sage wasn't disappointed in how I kicked off her New Year either.

CHAPTER 14

Sage

"I'LL SEE YOU WHEN YOU GET HOME LATER TONIGHT."

My hands slid over Gunner's shoulders and around his neck. After he pressed a kiss to my cheek, I replied, "Okay. Have a good day at work."

"You too."

I thought Gunner would give me another kiss and leave, but he didn't. He just stood there holding me in his arms, looking at me with such adoration and love.

"What's going on?" I asked.

Instead of answering me immediately, Gunner searched my face. I gave him the time to do it, mesmerized by the look in his eyes. Eventually, he spoke. And when he did, his voice was so soft and gentle.

"Good news today."

At those words, I finally understood why he was looking at me the way he had been.

Wetness filled my eyes as I agreed, "Yeah."

At that, Gunner closed the distance between our faces and captured my mouth with his. As his tongue swiped into my mouth, I felt not only the love he had for me, but also the relief at hearing today's news.

Once he'd successfully communicated that to me, he pulled back and buried his face in my neck. He kissed me there and hugged me tight to him. I held on just as tight.

When we separated, Gunner turned slightly toward the door and said, "Love you, Sage."

"I love you, too."

Not needing another exchange between us, Gunner left.

I stood there staring at the door for a few moments, my hand resting protectively on my growing abdomen. As I stroked my hand over the bump, I couldn't help but feel immense gratitude and love for Gunner and what he'd given me.

It was the end of January, and I was just over twenty weeks pregnant. Early this morning, Gunner and I went to our twenty-week scan for the baby. I don't think either of us had really taken the time to think about this part of the pregnancy. The truth was that this whole relationship had been a whirlwind from the start. It was hard to keep up with all the changes.

But over the last week, Gunner and I both started worrying just a little bit. That didn't necessarily mean that we didn't worry at all in the weeks leading up to this point. It was just that so many other things had been consuming our thoughts for the first half of the pregnancy, such as work, the holidays, our new relationship, and the news that we were even going to be parents.

As the time closed in on this morning's appointment, it started to hit us what the purpose of the more in-depth scan was. Obviously, checking on the baby's growth was part of it, but we knew that if there were any problems with the baby's development, we'd likely find out at this appointment.

So, the relief Gunner felt this morning was nothing more than knowing that we'd gotten good news. Our baby was healthy and his or her development was right on track. There wasn't even a situation where the doctor had any specific areas that he wanted to keep an eye on.

While I knew that Gunner and I were both concerned about what this ultrasound would bring today, I don't think it was until this moment that I realized just how worried Gunner had been. It made me fall in love with him that much more.

Now, he'd gone to work, and I had to force myself off the spot I was in to get myself ready to do the same. As much as I wanted to stay home and wait for Gunner to return, I couldn't. The last thing I wanted was to start using my paid time off unnecessarily.

So, I unstuck myself and went to get ready for work.

An hour and a half later, I was at work and my co-worker, Marissa, who was also one of the news anchors was bursting with happiness in front of me.

"Boy or girl?" she asked.

I shrugged.

Before I had the chance to say anything, she pressed, "You didn't find out?"

Shaking my head with a grin on my face, I confirmed, "Nope."

Marissa's eyes widened. "How are you doing that?" she wondered. "If I could have found out sooner than is possible, I would have. You're willingly waiting another twenty weeks?"

I couldn't help but laugh. "Well, if it makes you feel any better, it's all my decision," I began. "Gunner wanted to find out, but I didn't."

"He didn't fight you on it?" she asked.

"No. When they got to that part of the anatomy scan, they asked if we wanted to know. Gunner said yes at the same time I said no, and we had a bit of a standoff there," I told her.

Prior to the appointment, Gunner and I hadn't discussed

whether we'd find out the sex of the baby. When we were there, it suddenly became a topic of debate. He really wanted to find out, but I wanted to keep it a surprise.

He was genuinely shocked that I was willing to wait.

"Really?" he asked.

Nodding, I said, "Yeah."

"I thought you'd want to know if we're having a boy or girl," he remarked.

"I do want to know,' I assured him. "I just want to wait until the baby is here to find out."

He sat back a little and stared at me as the technician stood and walked to the other side of the room to give us a minute. I appreciated her willingness to wait patiently for us while we took the time to figure out what we were going to do.

"Is there anything I can do to change your mind?" he questioned me.

"Honestly, I don't think so. But if you really want to know, I'd be okay with you finding out ahead of me. If that's what you want, I don't want to take it away from you. For me, it's just that… well, everything has been a surprise with you."

When his brows pulled together, I explained, "I'm talking about everything between us. I was so surprised when I walked outside the news station that day and saw you there. Finding out we were having this baby and then getting your reaction… another surprise. I won't even get into the surprises I've had learning about the man that you are in so many different facets of our life together. Ultimately, in every single case, those surprises have turned out to be the best of my life. And life doesn't have enough good surprises. So, that's why I want to wait."

Gunner took a moment to consider my words. It didn't take him long to declare, "You're right. We've been doing well with the surprises. I've had quite a few of my own with you, and I'm learning that I love them. This will be just one more to add to the list."

"Are you sure? I'm more than okay with you learning the sex today if you promise to keep it a secret from me," I reiterated.

"I'm sure. We'll wait."

I grinned at him and reached up to touch his cheek. "It'll be worth it," I promised.

"Everything with you always has been," he replied.

A moment later, we called the technician back over and told her we were going to wait.

Now, it seemed my co-worker was just as shocked.

"Well, it looks like you won that battle," she noted.

"I guess you could say that, but it didn't really feel like a battle, to be honest," I told her.

And it didn't. Gunner and I didn't exactly fight about it. I truly would not have been upset if he wanted to find out the sex of the baby. He simply listened to my perspective and realized he was okay with waiting. Quite frankly, I thought the whole situation spoke volumes about our ability to communicate and compromise with one another. My wants and desires were no more important than his. Recognizing this was something that made me feel great. I believe the whole thing was a good indicator of how we'd handle any issues that would arise in the future.

"Well, whatever you end up with, it's going to change your life forever," Marissa started. "I almost forget what life was like before Emmett and I had Elijah. It's been wonderful."

Marissa and her husband had welcomed their first baby, Elijah, just over a year ago. Emmett was born before I started working at the station, so I never knew Marissa when it was just her and her husband. Regardless, according to her, motherhood was one of the greatest joys of her life. I looked forward to experiencing that same feeling.

"I can't wait," I shared. "Gunner and I are so excited. June can't come soon enough."

"It'll be here before you know it. How are you managing now that you're at the halfway point?"

"Really well. Considering how sick I was at the beginning of this, I feel like the growing belly is a welcome side effect," I joked.

"Your bump is so cute," she said. "That's literally the only thing that tells anyone you're pregnant. You look fantastic, Sage."

"Thanks, Marissa. I appreciate that."

Just then, Devin, Marissa's co-anchor walked up and noted, "It's just about that time. Are you ready?"

"Yep. I'll be right there," Marissa replied before turning her attention back to me. "You better get yourself ready for your report. They were saying there are a few snowstorms on the horizon."

I nodded. "Yeah. We're monitoring them closely, but safe to say that there's going to probably be a few people snowed in and kids staying home from school soon."

"Got to love it," she replied. "I'll see you out there."

After I dipped my chin in response, Marissa turned and walked off. At that, I got myself ready and got to work. And when I finally did start giving my report, I ended up doing it thinking about the man who'd be watching it and looking forward to the moment I got home to him.

I had just barely stepped in the house from the garage late that night when Gunner stood in front of me and slid his arms around my waist. He buried his face in my neck and kissed me there. I tilted my head back to give him easier access.

Mere moments passed when Gunner began stripping me out of my clothes. His hands went to my shoulders and pushed my jacket down my arms. It fell to the floor right there, just inside the door.

With his lips gently brushing up against mine, Gunner whispered, "So sexy, Sage." He continued to move his hands over my curves as he went on, "This dress has been my favorite one to watch you in."

I smiled inwardly, loving that he not only watched my weather reports but also appreciated the effort I put into giving him what I knew he loved.

After Gunner and I talked about the changes my body was going through and he made it clear that he loved it all, I decided to accentuate it. We'd shared the news of our pregnancy with everyone, so there was no longer any reason to conceal the growing evidence of it.

I knew that not every woman was lucky enough to have a man support them through every step of their pregnancy *and* have that man prove just how attracted he was to her given her weight gain. Gunner had no problems with any of that. And at a time like this, I really appreciated the fact that he was more than willing to communicate that to me.

"I feel like you say that to me about every dress I've worn over the last couple of weeks," I pointed out.

He smiled against my lips. "That's because I love seeing you in all of them. You're honestly the hottest woman I've ever laid my eyes on," he returned. "But as much as I love this dress on you, I'll like it a lot more on the floor."

"Well, Mama has had a long day on her feet, so you're going to have to pick up the slack tonight," I warned.

"Challenge accepted."

At that, Gunner was done talking. He shifted his body to my side, bent slightly, and lifted me in his arms. I couldn't even put into words what it meant that he could carry me like I weighed no more than a feather. Gunner climbed the stairs and took me to our bedroom. After gently placing me on my back in the center of our bed, he got to work on my shoes. He slipped them off my feet and dropped them to the floor. Then he was massaging my feet.

"Oh, I'm the luckiest woman in the world," I moaned.

Gunner chuckled. "This is just a teaser, stranger. You've got plenty more pleasure coming your way."

I closed my eyes and smiled, thoroughly enjoying the relief Gunner's hands were providing. I wasn't even thinking about any of the other good stuff that I knew was heading my way soon. Once he'd taken a substantial amount of time to massage my feet, he began kissing up my legs.

Gunner's mouth made it to just above my knees when he slid his hands under my dress and up my thighs. He pulled back just a touch so he could bring his eyes to mine. "Lift up," he urged.

I lifted my hips a touch while Gunner quickly pushed my dress over my ass. Resting on his shins between my legs, Gunner leaned forward as he slid the material off my belly. Then he kissed the skin there so gently I could just barely feel his lips. The sweet and tender way he touched and kissed my abdomen all the time made my heart melt.

He was going to be the best dad in the world.

Satisfied with the amount of attention he paid to my bump, Gunner continued to move up my body. Somehow, without any help from me, he managed to lift my torso enough to free the dress from behind my back and over my breasts. After whipping it over my head, he tossed it aside and brought his mouth to the top swells of my full breasts. He had one hand cupping the side of one of my breasts while the other hand stroked from my upper thigh to my hip.

Through this, Gunner was careful not to put any weight on my abdomen.

When he finished showering my breasts with attention, his hand slid up and curled around the side of my neck. I thought he was going to kiss me, but he didn't.

Instead, I was surprised to see him staring at me like I was some prize he'd won and never wanted to lose. I tried to return the look, but the intensity in his stare was too much.

"Gunner," I rasped.

"Thank you, Sage," he returned his odd reply.

I gripped his shoulder and asked, "Why are you thanking me?"

His thumb stroked slowly along my jaw as he searched my face. When he finally settled his gaze on my eyes, he admitted, "I'm not sure what else to say or do to let you know how grateful I am for you."

He was going to make me cry. The sincerity in his tone held an edge of despair. It was like he genuinely believed he was the lucky one.

"I feel the same, Gunner," I assured him. "You aren't alone."

He shook his head. "No, Sage. You don't understand. I'm not saying you don't appreciate me, but this is different. I sat here today when I got home from work and watched you on television. Seeing you there, working hard, wearing that dress was just too much after our appointment this morning. I can't begin to tell you how lucky I feel that I not only have you, but also that you are sacrificing every day to keep our baby safe and healthy. We got that news today because of you."

Tears filled my eyes. "Gunner…" I trailed off. When I composed myself enough to swallow past the lump that had formed in my throat, I insisted, "This is your baby, too. You have just as much of a part in it as I do."

He let out a small laugh. "That's hardly true," he debated. "You've given up space in your body. You've taken care of yourself, and you're not purposely doing anything to jeopardize the health and safety of our baby. I know there are things that are completely out of your control, but where it counts, you're doing everything you can. There's nothing I can do in this situation, and that's been hard to handle. I'm used to being in control, and over the last week, I started to worry about the things that were out of my hands. I did my best not to let it show so I didn't worry you, but it wasn't a good place to be."

"But you did have control," I argued. "You've had it from the very beginning."

He shot me a look of confusion. "How?" he asked.

"Every day that goes by," I started. "You make me feel good about myself and always put my needs ahead of your own. Just the simple fact that you kept your fears from me leading up to that appointment is a testament to that. It would have stressed me a bit to know that you were feeling worried, especially when I'm so used to you being so confident, and that wouldn't have been good for our baby."

Gunner didn't respond to my words, so I ordered, "Don't discount how important what you're doing is in all of this, Gunner. I might be going through the physical changes here, but you're the one handling all of the emotional stress. If you had walked away from me in the beginning and I didn't have you, I'm not sure I'd be doing this well. So, thank you. Thank you for being my pillar of strength from the very beginning."

Gunner's features softened. "I love you so much, Sage. I hate that I had to wait this long to have you like this in my life, but you've made it all worth it."

"I feel precisely the same way, handsome."

When he made no move to say or do anything, I called, "Gunner?"

"Yeah?"

"I need you to make love to me now," I said.

He didn't respond with words. But his hands and mouth did. Those were the only things I needed right then anyway.

And it was magical.

CHAPTER 15

Sage

"BREAKFAST TIME."

The sound of Gunner's voice first thing in the morning was something I'd grown to love. From the time he'd moved in with me when I was sick at the beginning of my pregnancy, he'd always gotten up early in the morning and gone downstairs to make breakfast for me. When the morning sickness subsided, Gunner didn't change his morning routine. He continued to bring me breakfast in bed every morning.

I rolled to my back and turned my head in the direction of his voice. When I opened my eyes, I saw him standing there holding two plates.

"Good morning," I said, the sleepiness still evident in my voice.

"Good morning," he replied.

After throwing the covers back from my legs, I swung my legs over to the side of the bed and got out. "Sorry, my bladder is full again."

Gunner laughed and said, "I'll wait until you get back."

I quickly strode past him toward the bathroom. Wanting nothing more than to join him back in bed for breakfast, I didn't dawdle. I emptied my bladder, washed my hands, and walked back into the bedroom.

"I swear, it's like that's become my second home," I mumbled, moving toward my side of the bed. Gunner had gotten himself settled on his side after he'd thoughtfully piled up my pillows on my side. "I feel like I spend more time in the bathroom all night long than I do actually in bed sleeping."

Once I climbed in, I pulled the cover back up over my legs. Then Gunner held my plate out to me. "Thank you," I said, taking it from him.

"You're welcome. And I'm sorry about the bathroom trips. I know it's not easy, and you aren't really getting a good night's rest because of it."

I shrugged. "I'll survive. It's really a small price to pay," I assured him, spearing my eggs with a fork. After taking my first bite and loving it, I sighed, "I'm going to be so sad once the baby is born."

The physical force of Gunner snapping his head in my direction could be felt in the bed. It concerned me, so I stopped lifting the second forkful mid-air and looked over at him.

"Why would you be sad about our baby being here?" he asked once he had my full attention.

Realizing why he was so upset, I reassured him, "I didn't mean that the way it came out, Gunner. I just meant that you spoil me so much right now since I'm pregnant. I'm going to miss breakfast in bed after he or she arrives. That's all I meant."

"Breakfast in bed isn't stopping after the baby is here," he insisted.

My brows shot up. "It's not?"

He shook his head and explained, "I think it's something I'll want to continue doing for a really long time."

"Really?" I asked.

Nodding, Gunner went on to completely rock my world more than he already had in all the months we'd been together. The sweetest look I'd ever seen crossed his face, and he shared, "I like waking up next to you, Sage. I'm not sure I'll ever forget the feeling of waking up after that first night we were together and not seeing you there beside me. So, I figure that as long as I wake up and you're there, I'm going to be more than happy to make you breakfast."

My heart.

I hadn't realized how badly he'd been affected by me leaving early that morning without waking him. It made me feel awful to think I'd caused that kind of heartache for him. I guess I could completely understand it, though. If I had woken up that morning and he had snuck out of my place without telling me, it would have hurt.

"I'm sorry I did that," I lamented. "It was wrong. I wouldn't have appreciated it if you had done the same to me."

Gunner held his toast in his hand and leaned toward me. After giving me a kiss on the cheek, he brushed it off. "It's okay, babe. I appreciate the apology, but I'm here with you now. That's really all that matters."

Just like that, Gunner moved on. He didn't hold a grudge or any animosity. Maybe it wasn't important now, but I honestly couldn't say that I'd be in the same headspace as him if the roles had been reversed.

"Are you sure?" I pressed.

"Positive."

I dipped my chin in acknowledgment before getting back to my food. For the next few minutes, Gunner and I both ate in silence. We often did that, not needing a constant stream of words between us. Sometimes, we just liked having the company of the other person without the pressure for conversation. I loved that we had that, too.

Today wasn't one of those days where I let the silence stretch for too long, though. I had finished my eggs and was nibbling on my toast when I asked, "How has work been lately for you? Any new and exciting cases?"

"It's been routine lately," he started. "I'm happy about that. We've dealt with a lot of crazy things over the last few years, so the fact that things have really calmed down for the past couple of months has been a welcomed change of pace. I've got no complaints."

"That's good."

"Yeah, it is," he agreed. "I'm just happy you and I haven't had any of the issues the rest of the guys have had with their women."

"What do you mean?"

Gunner snapped his lips together and didn't respond. I grew concerned and pressed, "What is it?"

"It's not all very nice. Are you sure you want to hear about it?" he returned.

I nodded. "Yes, of course."

"It started with Elle and Levi. She had an obsessed stalker who tried to kill her. After her situation was Lexi and Cruz. She was kidnapped and nearly thrown into the middle of a sex-trafficking ring. No sooner did that get solved when Dom and Ekko got together. She had already been through a ton of shit in her life. She didn't really need anything else, but she ended up getting kidnapped in the middle of a snowstorm by someone associated with an old case Dom worked on. Not long after that, Lorenzo and Jolie dealt with their own bit of drama. Jolie was a victim of a pre-meditated hit-and-run. Weeks later, she was nearly shot, but Lorenzo stepped in front of the bullet to protect her. Pierce and Zara got together next. Luckily, other than being burned by her ex, which forced her to move here, she didn't experience any life-threatening antics. She and Pierce were mostly tested because as she tried to work through her past hurts, he was investigating the string of arsons in town. They eventually made it through, though. Of course, the person affected by those fires was Leni. She and Holden ended up getting together, but that wasn't without its own challenges. Holden struggled a bit with their relationship and by the time he realized what he was giving up, it was almost too late. She was kidnapped and drowned in a pool. Tyson and Holden were thankfully able to rescue her and revive her. We thought it was finally all done, but then Tyson and Quinn got together. After getting divorced because her husband cheated on her with her best friend, she ended up being held at gunpoint for her jewelry that she makes. It's been a rollercoaster these last few years with all of it."

I sat there staring at Gunner, unable to comprehend everything he'd just told me. It wasn't that I was confused about any of what he said. I just couldn't believe that all of these people he worked with had experienced these horrific situations.

My silence must have gone on for too long because Gunner clipped, "Fuck. I'm sorry, Sage. I probably should have been a little less graphic with all of that."

I blinked several times, trying to clear the thoughts from my head. Once I'd accomplished that, I asked, "Is everyone okay?"

"Yes," he replied immediately. "Nobody has had any permanent side-effects from anything that happened. They've all recovered from their ordeals, whether physically, emotionally, or both."

"Wow," I marveled.

After a moment of hesitation, Gunner reasoned, "I'm guessing we experienced our situation at the beginning of our relationship when you were off chasing hurricanes."

I let out a laugh and rolled my eyes. "We weren't chasing hurricanes," I scolded him playfully.

"Whatever. It was ridiculous and scared the living daylights out of me," he said.

"I'm here now and I'm fine," I reminded him as I leaned in his direction.

He moved toward me and whispered, "Yeah, you are."

A moment before he was going to kiss me, my phone rang on the nightstand.

"Sorry," I lamented as I pulled away and reached out to grab it. I picked it up, saw the name on the display, and answered, "Hey, Marissa."

"Sage, are you okay?" she questioned me.

I was caught off guard by her odd greeting, so I replied cautiously, "Yeah. Why wouldn't I be?"

"I'm guessing you haven't checked your email or seen the station's social media pages, have you?"

Suddenly, my body froze. I didn't know what Marissa was referring to, but if it was something on the station's social media outlets and she was asking me if I was okay, I had a feeling it wasn't going to be good.

"No, I haven't. What's going on?"

There was a long pause before Marissa apologized, "I'm so sorry, Sage. This is awful."

"Marissa, just tell me," I demanded, growing more and more concerned and impatient.

Following another stretch of silence, she shared, "Apparently, there were a number of viewers watching last night that weren't happy with your attire. One person made an awful comment last night and it seems to have exploded overnight."

I wondered if perhaps something had been on my dress that nobody at the station noticed. Sure, it would have been embarrassing, but there were worse things in life. I knew that for a fact because Gunner had just rattled off a list of far more serious issues.

"I don't understand," I told her. "What was wrong with it?"

Marissa groaned. "I don't want to be the one to tell you this," she started. "But it's probably better that I tell you and you stay away from the internet for a few days."

"Marissa!" I cried, feeling beyond frustrated.

"Sorry. I'm sorry. It's just that… well… one woman commented on your dress and said that you looked disgusting with your belly showing. She strongly recommended that the station address your wardrobe and convince you to wear appropriate maternity clothing."

"Are you serious?" I asked.

"I wish I were joking. I feel so awful, Sage."

"It's fine," I assured her. And it was. I expected from time to time that I'd experience criticism from people. I was in the public eye, so to speak, and had prepared myself for disparaging comments. For that reason, I added, "One hateful person isn't going to ruin my day, Marissa."

"It's not one person," she shot back.

"What?"

"After that comment was posted, it started a discussion. There were tons of people agreeing with her. Of course, there were just as many people defending you. But you know how it is. We can hear all the praise in the world, and all we'll ever hear is that single critic. In this case, there are hundreds of critics."

Oh my God.

Hundreds?

Something that had been so exciting and positive in my life and in my relationship with Gunner was causing this much dissension. I needed to see it.

"I have to go," I told her.

"Sage, don't go online. We'll talk tonight when you—"

I cut her off and insisted, "I have to go now, Marissa."

Then, without waiting for a response, I disconnected the call.

Without another word, I scrambled out of the bed. As I ran from the room, I vaguely heard Gunner calling my name. I couldn't pay attention to that, though. I was too focused on my mission. I made it to one of the spare bedrooms I'd converted to an office, snatched my laptop up off the desk, and turned to move back toward my bedroom.

Apparently, I had been moving quickly because when I got there, Gunner had only made it to the door. He was looking more than slightly alarmed.

"Sage, babe, what's going on?" he worried.

I didn't respond. The tightness in my throat and the awful churning in my stomach wouldn't allow me to speak.

Sitting down on the bed, I opened the laptop and immediately went to one of the station's social media outlets. It didn't take long to locate the post.

Someone there needs to tell the weather girl about her dress. Nobody wants to see her disgusting stomach like that.

Directly beneath that comment was a reply from an individual who agreed.

Agreed! I don't even want to watch anymore. You're the one having the baby, Sage Thompson. Don't make the rest of us suffer along with you.

If that wasn't enough, the original poster replied and added more salt to the gaping wound.

Don't you just love the fact that she's clearly very pregnant, but there's no ring on her finger? She's not even married and she's flaunting that stomach like she's proud of being another single, unwed mother.

A third commenter didn't relent.

Back in my day, it used to be about modesty. It seems now that women will spread their legs for anyone. Knowing that, how can we expect that she'd wear proper maternity clothing that conceals her body. Oh, I guess the times have changed.

The stream of comments that followed did have some in there defending me or stating that they thought I looked adorable, but most were degrading. And just as Marissa said, no matter how many positive ones I read, the only thing I could focus on was the negative.

I lifted my gaze from the computer screen and saw Gunner standing at the foot of the bed staring at me. Tears instantly filled my eyes as my hand instinctively moved to my belly.

Was this what motherhood would be like? I thought.

I wondered if this was normal. Would I constantly feel the weight of other people's opinions like this? Or was this a unique situation?

"Sage?" Gunner called, his eyes dropping to my hand resting on my stomach. "Are you okay? Is the baby alright?"

My throat was still tight when I finally replied, "I would do anything to protect our child. Anything at all."

Gunner rounded the bed and sat down on the edge of it in front of me. "I know you would," he insisted. "Why are you telling me that? And why are you so upset?"

I swallowed hard, the sickening feeling not subsiding. I

didn't think I could repeat even one of the awful statements I'd read. So, I simply picked up the laptop and turned it around.

Gunner took it from me as I sat back against my pillows. Then I watched as he grew angrier and angrier. I wasn't sure how much time passed before he closed the laptop with a bit of force that indicated he was beyond pissed off. Once he set it aside, Gunner shifted his body up the side of the bed until he was sitting right beside my hip. The moment his eyes connected with mine, the anger was gone and his features had softened.

"The only opinions you need to worry about, Sage, are yours and mine. Even mine is debatable, but considering I only have positive and encouraging things to say to you because they are the truth, mine should count for something."

He lifted his hand to my cheek and pleaded, "Please, honey, don't let them get inside your head. They don't deserve any space there. You are beautiful. Your body is beautiful. And our baby is a miracle. There is nothing for you to feel ashamed about."

I nodded slowly. Of course, I knew that everything he was saying was accurate, but it still stung to know so many people said such hurtful and hate-filled things in their comments.

"You and I know what we have between us," he went on. "They're all just making ignorant assumptions and being judgmental. You have to promise me you're going to ignore it."

"I'll try," I told him.

"Promise me, Sage," he begged. "Promise me you won't listen to their nastiness."

As a tear rolled down my cheek, I said, "I don't want to, Gunner. But that was a lot to take in. If it were just me, I don't think it'd bother me as much. But they're talking about our baby. Our baby isn't disgusting, Gunner."

"Of course not," he agreed. "Some people are just miserable. But you told me you would do anything to protect our child. I need you to follow through on that right now by not allowing this to weigh so heavily on your mind. Stress like this isn't going to help you or our little one."

"I know. I promise I'm going to try to ignore it. I don't know if I'll be successful, but at least I'm going to try."

His thumb stroked over my cheek, wiping away my tears. "That's my girl," he praised me.

When he leaned closer and touched his mouth to mine, I wondered if I'd be successful in my endeavor. I never expected I'd ever receive this kind of backlash in my career, let alone over the fact that I was having a baby.

Just thinking of it like that had me wanting to sit up a little taller.

I was having a baby.

I was doing something that so many women didn't have the privilege of doing. There was no way I wasn't going to try my very hardest to embrace and love each and every part of the process.

In fact, I had every intention of marching into work later this afternoon wearing another dress that not only made me feel great but also made the man whose opinion I cared about crazy for me.

This was going to be a little hiccup in the road. Everyone surely will have gotten it out of their system and will move on. Giving in was not going to be an option. I'd stick to my guns and do what made me feel good.

If they didn't like it, that was too bad for them.

CHAPTER 16

Sage

THERE WAS NOTHING LIKE A COMFORTING EMBRACE FROM A friend, especially in a situation like this.

The minute I walked into work, Marissa came toward me and pulled me into her arms without a word. We stayed like that for a long time without a single verbal exchange. It felt good to have her support.

When we separated, she put her hands to my shoulders and asked, "Are you okay?"

Nodding, I replied, "Yeah. Thanks for calling me earlier."

"I felt so awful once I realized that you didn't know. I mean, we know it's my job to report the news, but that's not something I ever want to do again," she returned.

The irony of the situation made me laugh. Until she pointed it out, I hadn't realized that it had been like that.

"It's really okay, Marissa," I assured her. "Gunner and I talked about it this morning. He made me realize that some people can be miserable and that I can't let it get to me. I'll admit I did look at some of the comments people were making. I should have listened to you and stayed away from that. It kind of sent me spiraling for a little bit. Luckily, I had a great guy there to help me work through it."

"I wish you had listened to me and not looked at it," she started. "It was difficult for me to read, and it wasn't even about me."

"Yeah, you and me both," I put in. "But I promise I'm good now. I'm going to do my best to ignore it. If these people don't get a reaction from me or anyone else at the station, I'm sure they'll just go away."

"I hope so."

After a brief pause, I tilted my head to the side and asked, "How was it for you?"

Marissa's brows pulled together. "What do you mean?" she shot back.

"When you were pregnant," I clarified. "Did you deal with negative comments from strangers all the time when you were pregnant with Elijah and on the air?"

Nervously biting her lip, Marissa slowly shook her head.

I blinked in surprise. "Not at all?" I wondered.

"No. That's what I don't understand. I actually thought this was the best place to work at that time given how supportive the viewers were. Honestly, I can't even remember receiving a single comment that was negative. Everyone was overwhelmingly supportive," she told me.

Hearing that shocked me a bit. I was happy that Marissa hadn't dealt with such awful criticism surrounding her pregnancy, but it confused me. Why was I getting such grief? Unfortunately, I had a feeling I already knew that there was likely a combination of reasons.

Not wanting to face that reality, I shrugged my shoulders, brushed it off, and reasoned, "Maybe it's because I'm the new kid in class. Once they realize their nastiness isn't going to affect me, they'll back off. I mean, that's got to be the only reason someone would go through that much trouble to comment repeatedly on something that has literally zero bearing on their life and circumstances."

"I hope you're right."

"Has anyone else here said anything about it?" I asked, wondering if perhaps I was going to end up having someone talk to me about needing to change my attire.

Marissa nodded and shared, "They're all mortified. Everyone feels so bad for you because we've honestly never received this type of criticism before about anything. I expect the rest of the staff is going to be extra nice to you now."

I let out a laugh. "And there's the silver lining," I noted. "Of course, it's not like everyone here hasn't always been nice to me anyway. But I'll accept whatever perks come from this mess."

"I'm proud of you, Sage," Marissa beamed. "You look amazing and you shouldn't have to hide such a blessing in your life simply because of a few bad apples. I already can't imagine how you must feel. If that had happened to me when I was pregnant with Elijah, I'm not sure if I would have been able to show my face here again. You such a strong woman. Bottom line, if you're comfortable, that's all that matters. The way some of those comments were written you'd think that you were wearing nothing at all."

My eyes widened at the thought. "Oh, I don't think you'll have to worry about that. Exhibitionism hasn't ever really been my thing. But even if I thought I needed to do something drastic to take a stand against this mob, I'm pretty sure it won't resort to that. My man would shut that down really quick," I teased. Looking down at the dress I was wearing, I added, "He might love seeing me on television wearing dresses like this, but I'm relatively certain he'd not want me sharing *that* much."

Marissa giggled and declared, "I'm so happy he supports you like that. I honestly can't wait to meet this guy."

It warmed my heart to know that my friend wanted to meet the man who made me happy. "I'm sure one day you will," I assured her.

She dipped her chin in acknowledgment before she urged, "We should probably get to work. Everyone might feel bad for you, but they still expect us to get our jobs done."

Laughing, I agreed, "Yeah. It's probably best I don't take advantage of the situation."

At that, Marissa and I ended our conversation and turned to walk away so we could get to work. As nice as it would have been to be able to get paid for chatting with my friend all day, I knew that wasn't an option. And considering the topic of our conversation wasn't necessarily a pleasant one at the root of it, I was happy to get to work and leave the negativity behind me.

Gunner
Seventeen weeks later

"So, it's all set then?"

"Yes, Mr. Hayes. Everything is confirmed."

"Perfect. Thank you."

I pulled the phone from my ear and set it down in the cradle on my desk. No sooner had I done that when Tyson walked in.

"Hey, man, how's it going?" he asked.

I sat back in my chair and answered, "I honestly can't complain. Life is really good right now."

Sitting down in the chair on the opposite side of my desk, he pointed out, "There's not much time left, is there?"

I shook my head. "Nope. I can't wait either," I stated.

Those were really the only words I could use to describe how I felt. Sage was thirty-five weeks pregnant, and we were mere weeks away from becoming parents and starting this new chapter in our lives. I was beyond excited for what was ahead for us.

"How's Sage managing?" he asked.

Sage. She was something else. I didn't know if it was possible to love her more than I already did. Never had I met a woman like her who could power through everything that had been thrown at her the last several months. Even though she had moments that were particularly difficult and trying for her, she still pressed on.

"More than anything else, she's growing more and more uncomfortable," I told him.

"What about the noise on the media?" he questioned me.

Shaking my head, feeling nothing but frustration, I admitted, "She's handling it better than I am."

"I can't imagine being in your shoes," he began. "If someone was saying stuff like that about Quinn, I'd lose my mind."

I nodded. "Yeah, I've all but done that. Sage is the only reason I've kept it together."

That was the truth. It was incredibly frustrating to sit back while people made such horrible and disgusting comments about the woman I loved. No matter how much I wanted to do precisely what Tyson said and lose my mind, I didn't. I wholeheartedly believed my priority needed to be focusing on keeping her happy and distracted from the negativity. It wasn't necessarily difficult to do that because when I was with Sage, everything else seemed to fade away anyway.

But I worried for her, particularly when I wasn't around her or when she was at work.

Sage had been doing a phenomenal job of trying to ignore the comments from the people on social media, but she wasn't exactly having a ton of luck. That surprised me. Because I'd seen her confidence shine through on so many occasions. I loved that about her, especially when she gave it to me when I least expected it.

And while I couldn't say her confidence had completely faltered, it was definitely waning. To anyone watching her weather reports on television, they'd never know. Even in the few times we got together with friends or family over the last couple of weeks, Sage was always pleasant and joyful.

But I saw it in the quiet moments with her. In the privacy of our home, she struggled not to feel the sting of the hurtful words being thrown at her. She carried herself with such grace and dignity in the face of adversity.

That was precisely the reason why I was doing something about it now. She needed to get away from it all so she could just focus on the very beautiful thing that was happening between us and in her body. Nothing needed to be distracting her from that.

"You'll get through it," Tyson assured me.

Nodding, I agreed, "Yeah, we will. I'm surprising her this weekend and taking her away on a little vacation."

Surprise manifested in his features. "Really? Is that safe this close to the end?" he asked.

"I'm not going far. Just taking her out to a cabin in the mountains two hours away," I explained. "I just want to do something to lift her spirits a bit."

"That'll be nice. Some quiet time together before the baby comes along," Tyson replied.

"I'm going to ask her to marry me," I told him.

"No shit?" he responded, evidently even more shocked.

I shook my head and confirmed, "No joke. I've been wanting to do it for so long, but it never seemed like the right time. I'm surprised I lasted this long, though. On top of all the negative comments Sage has gotten surrounding the way she dresses on air, she's gotten a lot of flak about the fact that she's pregnant and not married. Obviously, I don't give a shit what anyone thinks about that, but she shouldn't have to take that on her shoulders, too. That's where I've been struggling. That day I first saw what people were saying, I nearly blurted out the question. Somehow, I managed to hold back from saying anything, which is good because I didn't have a ring then and she deserved something special. But the truth is, as you already know, I've wanted to propose to her since long before all this happened."

"Well, congratulations, man. That's awesome," Tyson said.

I let out a laugh. "Thanks. Now I just have to hope and pray she says yes."

"Do you think it's a possibility that she won't?" he asked.

"I'd like to think it's not an option. But she's pregnant and hormonal... anything could happen."

Tyson burst out laughing. When he got it under control, he didn't say anything that made me feel better about the situation. "You're right. Between my sisters and my sister-in-law, I know just as much as the next guy how that kind of stuff goes. Good luck. I'll be pulling for you."

"Thanks, Tyson. I appreciate it."

He dipped his chin, but before he could say anything, I asked, "Are you ready for your wedding?"

"The wedding? No. Being married to Quinn? Yes."

Now it was my turn to laugh. "That stressful?" I asked.

He shrugged. "I'll do whatever she wants, but all the frills don't matter to me either way. I just want her."

"I get it," I mumbled.

I completely understood where he was coming from. When it came to doing what I planned to do this weekend, the only thing that mattered to me was being with Sage for the rest of our lives. How that happened didn't really matter to me. I'd leave it up to her to decide and do whatever I could to help her with it.

"Well, I better get back to work," Tyson declared.

"Yeah, me too. I guess we should consider ourselves lucky," I said.

"What makes you say that?" he wondered.

"It's been quiet here at work lately," I started. "Obviously, we've got all the standard, run-of-the-mill private investigator stuff to deal with, but the craziness we've dealt with over the last few years seems to have come to an end. It's been nice to not feel so on edge about these horrific threats coming to people we know and care about."

"You can say that again," he muttered as he stood and walked toward the door. When he made it there, he turned and looked back at me. "Good luck this weekend."

A moment after I gave him a nod, he walked out.

Then, I sat there feeling distracted by and excited about my plans for this weekend just a little longer before I got back to work on a routine case.

"Check this and make sure everything you need for the next two-and-a-half days is here."

Sage's eyes went from mine to the bag on the bed and back again.

"What?" she asked.

Sage had just gotten home from work about thirty minutes ago. The minute she walked through the door, I met her there, kissed her, and urged her to get in the shower by telling her I had a surprise for her when she finished.

She'd just gotten out of the shower and walked into the bedroom. Before she made it home, I had gone through and packed up a few things for her. As sure as I was that I had everything there that she'd need, I didn't want to risk not having something she'd want. So I asked her to check the bag. She was, obviously, completely stunned.

"I'm taking you on a little trip," I explained. "I've packed your bags, but I might have forgotten something."

Something shifted in Sage's face, but she didn't respond. Without another word, she walked toward the bed, rummaged through the bag, and lifted her gaze to my face. "It's all there," she said. "Where are we going?"

I'd paid attention to everything about Sage since the very beginning. While I could have been wrong, I was mostly confident that I'd gotten everything. Of course, my career choice made it so I was just accustomed to noticing things, but I knew that that wasn't what this was. It was just Sage. I wanted to know everything there was to know about her. What she liked. What she disliked. And everything in between.

I grinned at Sage and replied, "It's a surprise."

"Will I be back on time for work on Monday?" she asked.

"Yes," I promised. "We'll be back before your bedtime on Sunday evening."

"Are we driving?" she pressed for more information.

Nodding, I confirmed, "I wasn't going to take you

somewhere on a plane this close to the end of your pregnancy. We'll be driving. This will feel like a mini-vacation, but it'll still be close enough that if you went into labor, we should still be able to get to the hospital on time."

She dipped her chin and agreed, "Okay. Take me away, handsome."

Just like that, Sage put her trust in me to take care of her. I couldn't help but think that if she was willing to do that now, she'd agree to allow me to do that for the rest of our lives.

Before she had the opportunity to change her mind, I gathered up her bag, took her by the hand, and led her out of the room.

Ten minutes later, we were on our way to what was going to be our first and last solo vacation. Or, at least, what was likely to be that for the foreseeable future.

CHAPTER 17

Sage

IT WAS OFFICIAL.

I was the luckiest woman in the world.

For months now it had been made clear to me through Gunner's actions just how great of a guy he was, but this irrevocably proved it.

"This is just what I needed," I sighed.

I was curled up on the couch with Gunner in a cabin in the mountains. It was mid-April, and in northwestern Wyoming, that meant it was still pretty chilly. For that reason, the roaring fireplace in front of us was perfect for taking the chill out of the air.

"No, I'm sorry. That's not right," I started. "I think this is just what *we* needed."

The look on Gunner's face softened. "Yeah," he agreed. "I thought it would be great for us to get away for a little bit."

I looked down my body, over my rounded belly, to where my legs were draped across Gunner's lap. His hands were massaging my legs and feet. That was another thing that proved my assumptions about him correct. He'd been diligent about providing me with massages. He did them well and often.

It didn't seem to matter to Gunner that he'd planned this

whole trip, worked all week, packed our bags, and drove us the two hours here while I napped in the car beside him. He continued to give me the very best of him. I felt extraordinarily grateful for him.

"This really means a lot to me," I told him. "Though, to be honest, there isn't much you've done since we got together that doesn't mean a lot to me."

He smiled at me and shared, "I had been thinking about this for a little bit. Obviously, it's no surprise that we haven't exactly had what most people might consider a traditional courtship. It dawned on me that you and I haven't really had an opportunity to take a trip alone. For that reason, I wanted us to do something—even something small like this—before the baby arrives."

I cocked an eyebrow and insisted, "This is not something small."

Gunner looked confused. "Sage, babe, we're a mere two hours away from home. And we're only going to be here for little more than two days. I would have loved nothing more than to take you on a proper vacation, but with you being so close to the end of the pregnancy, it's just too risky."

"That's where you're wrong, handsome," I started. "It's not about where we go or how long we're gone that makes this special. It's just about the two of us being together. And at a time like this, when we're about to embark on the biggest journey of our lives, this isn't something to just dismiss as though it's nothing. It's big and important, Gunner… and it means the world to me."

Gunner moved his hands from my left leg to my right and began working the sore, tired muscles there.

"I'm glad you feel that way, Sage," he replied, a touch of despondency in his tone.

I didn't want to ruin a perfectly good start to our weekend, but I also thought it was important to address the fact that it seemed there was still something bothering him.

Without really thinking about it, I blurted, "Do you regret it?"

His head snapped in my direction. "Regret what?" he asked.

"The way things progressed between us," I answered.

Gunner's immediate reaction was something that I was certain could be felt all the way back to Windsor. His whole body went solid as his hands stopped moving on my leg. I suddenly realized that he must have misinterpreted the meaning behind my question.

Wanting to clear up any confusion, I backtracked a bit and clarified, "Gunner, I'm not suggesting that you regret our baby. I know you don't."

"Do you?" he asked. "Do you regret our baby? Do you regret me?"

Terror flooded my veins. Somehow, it fueled a burst of energy that allowed me to swing my legs from his lap so I could sit up straighter and move my body closer to his.

"Not at all," I deadpanned. My voice dropped to just a touch over a whisper as I pleaded, "Please tell me you don't actually believe that."

"I didn't, but I don't understand where you're going with this," he responded.

The anguish in his voice was like a physical blow to my chest. My heart hurt knowing I'd caused him to sound like that.

Talk about regret.

I had to fix this. So, I brought a hand up to cup his cheek and explained, "Maybe I shouldn't have used the word regret.

That was a poor choice. I was just simply wondering if you ever thought about how things would be between us if I hadn't gotten pregnant."

"No, I haven't," he insisted. "I've loved every single minute of this journey with you. It's been the best thing that's ever happened to me."

Gunner's words made me feel good inside, but the husky tone of his voice had my heart breaking all over again. Though it felt like I had a boulder lodged in my throat, I knew I needed to find a way to speak past it.

Before I had a chance to do that, Gunner questioned me. "Do you think about what life would have been like had we not gotten together that first night?"

"I've never questioned us getting together that first night," I promised him. "Honestly, I've never really thought about any of this until just now. It's just that... well, with what you were saying about us not having more time to do things that most couples get to do before a child is thrown into the mix, I started to wonder if maybe that was bothering you. I didn't mean to imply that you were in any way upset about the fact that we're here now."

Gunner's eyes searched my face. I didn't know if he was trying to figure out what to say in response or if he was trying to decide if I was being honest with him. Eventually, he stated, "I might regret one thing."

That wasn't the response I had been expecting. My lips parted in shock at his words as my body tensed.

A moment later, Gunner said, "I should have asked you out back when we were in high school."

The air rushed from my lungs as I realized I'd suddenly stopped breathing. I'd barely regained my composure when he continued, "For a bunch of reasons that no longer matter, I didn't do that. But we're here now, Sage. I fully believe this was the life we were meant to have, and I wouldn't change a thing about it. I don't regret you, this baby, or any of the things that most people might be upset about missing out on."

Tears that had filled my eyes spilled down my cheeks. I dropped my head to Gunner's chest as his arms immediately came around me. The second I felt the comfort of his embrace, I burst into tears.

"I'm so sorry," I cried. "I never should have said that to you."

As one of his hands stroked up and down my back, he said, "It's okay, Sage. Just breathe."

"I love you, Gunner. Please tell me you know that," I begged through my tears.

His fingers drove into my hair, gripped it at the back of my head, and gave a gentle tug so I had no choice but to lift what I was sure was my red, splotchy, tear-stained face from his chest to look at him. Once he had my eyes, he assured me, "I know you love me, Sage."

I continued to stare at him as he brought his opposite hand up to wipe away my tears.

"This is supposed to be a good time for us," he started. "I don't like that you're crying right now."

"I feel horrible for insinuating that you were ashamed of us and where we are," I murmured.

"Stop feeling that," he ordered. "I understand why you asked. The minute you explained it, I understood. It was partly my fault for saying why I planned this trip the way I said it. So, I'm sorry, too, for putting that thought in your head. Please stop crying."

I dropped my head to his chest again, gripped his shirt in my hands, and took in a deep breath.

"That's it," he encouraged me. "Just breathe."

That's just what I did for the next few minutes. Gunner and I stayed there like that as I worked to calm myself down. Being this close to the end of my pregnancy, I didn't want to do anything to send myself into pre-term labor.

After some time had passed, Gunner asked, "Are you okay now?"

I shifted slightly on the couch, tipped my head back to look at him, and nodded. "Yeah. I'm okay now."

"How about we head to bed?" he suggested. "It's late and you've had a long day."

"Okay," I agreed.

With that, Gunner stood from the couch first before he turned and helped me up. Then we walked through the cabin to the bedroom where I thought we'd officially call it a night. But somehow, despite how busy the day had been, I wasn't completely ready for bed. Of course, I knew that meant I was going to have to do a little bit of coaxing to get Gunner to give me what I wanted.

The truth was, as my pregnancy progressed, Gunner made it very clear to me that he was still very attracted to me but preferred that I be the one to take the lead until after the baby was born. He didn't want me to feel pressure to have sex with him when I might not have been feeling up to it. Of course, he certainly made it easy for me to quickly get into the mood when he'd kiss me senseless or say sweet things to me. Tonight, though, I knew it was all going to be on me. Once I dropped the hint, he'd do what he loved to do and take over. And he'd have no problems with the fact that he would need to incorporate a bit of strategy and creativity to make love to me.

After we climbed into bed, I rolled to my right side to face him.

"You need to be on your left side, Sage," he told me, knowing that it was better for the baby if I was on my left side.

"I know, but I was just thinking that I wasn't exactly ready for bed," I said as I put a hand to his chest and started trailing my fingers over his skin. Gunner never wore a shirt to bed, and yet he always managed to remain so warm. He was like my own personal furnace.

He put his hand to my hip, gave me a gentle squeeze, and asked, "Are you sure?"

"Yes," I answered, my hand trailing down his abdomen. "I feel like it's been a little too long since I've last had you."

He chuckled and reminded me, "It was two days ago."

"That's a long time for a woman with this many hormones coursing through her body," I reasoned. "It's probably the equivalent of going like a month without it while not being pregnant."

"A month?" he questioned me.

"A month," I repeated.

"Well, I better do something about that," he surmised just before his lips pressed against mine and his hand went from my hip and into my panties so he could grab my ass. Since I had only been wearing one of his t-shirts and a pair of panties, he had easy access.

His tongue drove into my mouth, taking our kiss to that next level. With each swipe of his tongue or caress of his hands on my body, I found myself growing more and more turned on. Of course, my hormones had been doing a number on me lately, so it wasn't like I needed a whole lot of help in that area anyway.

Gunner's kisses were phenomenal, but I wanted more. So, I reluctantly tore my mouth from his, pressed my hand into his shoulder, and urged him to his back. His head was elevated by a mound of pillows, which I knew was going to be perfect for what I had planned.

I managed to get myself upright so I could slide my panties down my legs. Then I put my hands to either of Gunner's shoulders and swung my leg over him. His hand went between my legs.

"Soaked," he growled. "I love how hot you get for this, Sage."

"It's because it's you," I told him. "Help me, please."

Gunner knew what I needed and positioned himself so all I needed to do was sink down onto him. As soon as I did, I dropped my head back and moaned. Gunner didn't force me to move; he never did. But he brought his hands to the hem of his shirt I was wearing and whipped it over my head. No sooner was it gone when his hands came to my breasts and his mouth closed over one of my nipples.

"Yes," I moaned again.

This was just what I wanted… his face right in line with my breasts. They'd always been sensitive during sex for me, but now they were even more so. And I loved it.

As Gunner licked, sucked, and squeezed my breasts, I moved my hips over his length. I started slowly at first, but it didn't take me long to work up a rhythm. The man underneath me expertly worked my breasts while occasionally allowing a hand to drop down to my ass or thighs. I loved the feel of his hands on my body. Gunner knew it and was sure to use that knowledge to his advantage. Because while there was the obvious benefit to me of feeling his hands caressing my skin, there was also a benefit to Gunner. As I grew more and more turned on, I moved my hips faster. That is where he reaped his reward.

At the beginning of my pregnancy, I thought our sex life

would eventually start to suffer. Luckily, not only did it not ever suffer, I honestly believed it improved.

I didn't know if it was because we made the effort to do it regularly that I was able to still move relatively easy with my rounded belly, but my pace had picked up substantially. It always did when I was on the verge.

Gunner always knew it was happening, too. So, like always, he began to work my breasts harder. His tongue flicked faster over my nipple on one side while his finger did the same on the other side.

Seconds later, my breathing had grown labored and shallow. I didn't slow my pace, and before I knew it, I was crying out as the force of my orgasm tore through my body. As the final waves of it left me, my forehead dropped to Gunner's shoulder.

"Are you spent?" he asked.

"My hips are toast. I just need to get out of this position," I said. "Then you can take me however you want me."

He let out a chuckle and brought his hands to my hips. After giving me a few squeezes to help the soreness there, he helped me lift myself up and off to the side. A moment later, he was up on his knees behind me, pressing the tip of his hard cock at my opening. I put my hands to the top of the headboard and pushed back into him.

Gunner groaned and gripped my hips tighter in his hands. From that point forward, he took control. He powered into me relentlessly. At one point, he kept a hand on my hip while the other reached forward to hold my breast.

"Let go of the bed," he instructed.

I did as he asked and was instantly pulled upright, my back against his front. Gunner continued to thrust into me as his hands continued to caress my body.

"I'm going to come again," I warned him.

"Wait," he ordered.

I didn't think I could.

"No, please," I begged.

"Wait for me, Sage," he bit out, continuing to power into me.

He was crazy if he thought he could do that and I'd be able to hold myself back.

"I can't, Gunner," I insisted. "Please, you—"

Before I could finish my statement, Gunner cut me off and demanded, "Let it go, babe."

So, I did.

And because Gunner did too, it made my second orgasm far more pleasant than the first. It wasn't nearly as powerful but substantially more enjoyable.

After Gunner let go of me and helped me out of the bed, I moved to the bathroom to get myself cleaned up.

When I came back to the bed, he curled up behind me and held me close.

"Better?" he asked.

"Much," I confirmed.

With that, he pressed a kiss to my shoulder and said, "Goodnight, Sage."

"Goodnight, Gunner. I love you."

"Love you too."

By the time I fell asleep that night, I no longer had any concerns about Gunner's headspace.

I felt the bed dip behind me mere seconds before Gunner's hand came to my side and slid around to my belly. Cradling me there, he brought his mouth to my ear and whispered, "I brought you breakfast."

I smiled as I leaned back into him and joked, "Boy, do you know how to turn a girl on."

The bed shook with the force of Gunner's laughter, and I twisted my neck to watch him. I loved seeing him like that.

He moved his hand to my arm, kissed me on the cheek, and asked, "You want to use the bathroom first?"

After I sat up, I nodded and replied, "Yeah."

A couple minutes later, I was back in the bed with Gunner and we were eating breakfast together. Today he had made pancakes.

"Was this place stocked with food?" I asked.

He shook his head. "I brought some stuff with us. When we got here last night and you went in to use the bathroom, I unpacked all the groceries I'd picked up while you were still at work yesterday."

"So, he plans secret trips, gives massages, makes breakfast, *and* grocery shops?" I started. "Gosh, I better make sure I do everything I can to hold on to you."

"You could say yes," he returned.

Confused by his statement, I looked over after putting a forkful of pancake in my mouth and asked, "What do you mean?"

Gunner looked away as he set his plate down in his lap. He reached an arm out to the bedside table before he returned his attention to me. It was then I saw what he'd gotten off the table because Gunner held out a ring box and opened it up in front of me.

With a gorgeous shining diamond on display, he proclaimed, "You've made me the happiest man in the world, Sage. I love you more than I could even begin to put into words. But

I'd love the opportunity to try and show you what you mean to me for the rest of our lives. Will you marry me?"

I was shocked into silence. My eyes darted back and forth between Gunner's face and the ring box he held in his hand. When I finally settled them on his eyes, I noticed a bit of worry there and knew I needed to find my voice.

"Yes," I rasped. "Yes, I'll marry you."

Relief swept through him as Gunner immediately engulfed me in his arms and pulled me toward him. I did my best to keep my plate of pancakes steady as I lowered it to my lap. After I set it down, I hugged Gunner in return and held on tight.

He didn't let go for a long time, and I loved that he didn't. Following a minute or so of silence, he said, "I was starting to think you were going to say no."

"Never," I returned. "I feel like I've been waiting for this moment my whole life. In fact, I was beginning to think you didn't want to get married."

That caused Gunner to finally loosen his hold on me. When he was looking at me again, he said, "You aren't serious."

Nodding, I assured him, "I am. You haven't really ever talked about it."

"I told you I was going to make this the best year of your life," he reminded me. "What did you think I meant by that?"

"I know you said that, but then you never specifically mentioned marriage. Once all of that stuff started happening with the station's social media and all of the criticism I was getting, I thought it would have pushed you to want to ask right away. But you didn't, so I thought you were simply content to keep things the way they were."

"If I asked you all those weeks ago would you have said yes?" he questioned me.

"I would have said yes the day I got back from North Carolina after those hurricanes," I told him. "I was so terrified that you were going to walk away once you knew that I was pregnant. It broke my heart to think that I'd no longer have you."

Apparently, I'd shocked Gunner into silence because he sat there staring at me for a long time without saying any words. I gave him time to come to grips with whatever was going through his mind. As soon as he processed it, I knew he'd speak.

I was wrong.

Because Gunner didn't speak.

Instead, he pulled the ring out of the box, took my left hand in his, and slid the ring down over my knuckle to the base of my finger. The both of us sat there and stared at it while Gunner continued to hold my hand in his. The ring was the most beautiful ring I'd ever seen, and I wasn't saying that simply because it was the one currently adorning my finger.

"It's beautiful," I said softly. "It's the most perfect ring I've ever seen."

"Quinn custom-made it for you," he shared. "I told her what I wanted for you, and she did exactly what I asked."

"I love it." I lifted my gaze from the ring to Gunner and added, "I love you."

"I love you, too."

When I made no move to do anything else, Gunner leaned forward, touched his lips to mine, and initiated a kiss that lasted a long time. It started off as mostly sweet and innocent to start, but quickly turned spicy. Thankfully, Gunner had a bit of sense about him, so after he'd sufficiently kissed me and gotten me all hot and bothered, he ordered, "Finish your breakfast, Sage. We've got some celebrating to do."

I smiled at him and grabbed my fork. Just before I put another bite in my mouth I asked, "Is that what we'll be doing for the next two days?"

Gunner answered me with a dip of his chin and a devious grin.

CHAPTER 18

Sage

There wasn't much that was going to ruin my mood.

The fact that it was Monday afternoon, Gunner and I had returned from our mini-getaway yesterday evening, and that I was currently on my way to work couldn't put a damper on all the happiness I was feeling.

As I drove to the place that had been a source of contention for me the past few weeks, I thought on all I had to be grateful for. Sure, I'd been having a bit of a rough time with the negative criticism I'd been receiving from more than a handful of viewers, but I was putting it all behind me.

For the first few weeks after it was brought to my attention, I religiously checked the comments on our news feeds. Then I realized I was doing more harm than good, so I stopped. But it did little to help me forget just how awful people had been toward me.

After this weekend with Gunner, though, I was riding a high from which not even the nastiest of comments could knock me down.

I was engaged.

To my high school crush.

And we were expecting a baby in just over a month.

Gunner Hayes had rolled into my life without warning and revived my aching, lonely heart.

Nothing was going to diminish that.

With a smile on my face, I pulled into the parking lot at work. A few minutes later, I was inside searching for Marissa. I wanted to share the good news with her.

As I stepped inside the break room to put my dinner and snacks in the fridge, I found Marissa on her way out.

"Hey, Sage, how's it going?" she greeted me.

"Great," I beamed. "How was your weekend?"

"So relaxing," she started. "Well, as relaxing as it can be with a toddler. Mostly, I just mean that we didn't have anywhere to go or anything to do. It was such a nice break."

Nodding, I replied, "It sounds amazing."

"It was. What about you? What did you do this weekend?" she asked.

After putting my food in the refrigerator, I closed the door and walked toward her. I threw a hand out nonchalantly and said, "Oh, you know, nothing too crazy. I just got home from work on Thursday night and was surprised with a mini-vacation by Gunner. We went up to a cabin in the mountains. And on Friday morning, he proposed."

I held my left hand out to her. Her eyes dropped to the gorgeous ring, widened, and came back to meet mine.

"Holy crap, that thing is huge!" she declared. She took about half a second to stare at it again before she closed the distance between us and engulfed me in a hug. "Congratulations, Sage! That is so exciting!"

"Thank you," I returned. "It was truly the best weekend ever."

"I'll bet," she said. "Did you guys set a date?"

I shook my head. "Not yet. We've managed to finish

getting the baby's nursery done, but I still don't feel one hundred percent prepared for the baby. I need to focus on that right now. The only thing we're certain of with regard to a wedding is that we want to wait until after our little one arrives."

Nodding, she agreed, "That's a good idea. A newborn will be enough to keep you busy for a while. You guys will eventually figure it all out, though."

"Yeah. On the bright side, I'm hoping this will help with all of the negativity we've been seeing from those viewers," I told her.

Disappointment washed over her. "Honestly, they really should just keep their comments to themselves. I know we aren't going to be that lucky, though. I'd be willing to bet money that even though they'll see that ring on your finger, because it would be impossible for them to miss it given just how massive it is, they'll still find something to criticize."

I shrugged my shoulders. "Well, there's nothing I can do about that. If they want to be miserable that's their prerogative. I'm engaged to be married to the guy I've liked since high school. I don't really care what else they have to say."

With an approving nod, she stated, "Good for you."

If I was being honest with myself, it wasn't easy for me to get to this point. For a while I'd been doing my best to ignore it all, but I would have been lying if I said that deep down it didn't bother me. It really wasn't until this weekend that I had a breakthrough.

After pancakes and our first celebration of our engagement early Friday morning, I had some time to put things into perspective. I managed some of it on my own and the rest with the help of Gunner.

Once I'd gotten myself out of bed that morning, I got dressed and went out to sit on the covered balcony while

Gunner hopped in the shower. As I sat there staring out at the breathtaking scenery, it hit me.

I had a man who loved and cared about me in ways nobody ever had before him. His love for me ran so deep, it went far beyond the size of the ring on my finger or the location of the trip he'd brought us on.

It was just him being the man he was. Someone who loved me and cared about me with everything inside him.

It was about waking up and making me breakfast every morning and enjoying doing it.

It was about wanting to move in with me from the beginning of the pregnancy so he wouldn't miss a moment of it.

It was about giving me a massage after a long day.

It was about Gunner being the man he promised himself years ago he would be when the opportunity arose.

I felt incredibly lucky to be on the receiving end of his love.

And just as he walked outside to sit beside me, I realized that those who felt it necessary to make comments about me and the choices I made in my personal life or with my wardrobe were just missing something in their own lives. Something that I'd gotten when I got Gunner.

Before he sat down, Gunner leaned over, kissed me, and asked, "Are you cold?"

That right there was more proof of what I had with him.

I smiled as my heart swelled with love for him and replied, "No. I'm good."

He nodded and planted himself in the chair beside mine. He'd barely gotten himself settled when he spoke.

"I knew I wanted to ask you to marry me when you were out in North Carolina," he blurted.

I had barely enough time to let that sink in when he

continued, "But then you told me about the baby, and I didn't want you to think if I'd done it at any point from then on that I was asking simply out of obligation. So, I decided to wait a little while to give us some time to adjust to all the new things that were happening between us with the pregnancy, moving in together, and holidays with our families. Once that madness passed us, the whole thing happened with work for you. I wanted to ask you then, especially once people started questioning your morals. But you handled yourself so well, and I'm so proud of you for that. Ultimately, I decided that I needed to stop making excuses for not asking you and I just needed to do it. Nobody else needed to factor in my decision, just like nobody else factored into my decision that first night I met you at the station."

I reached my hand out to his. After our fingers were linked between us, I said softly, "This was perfect. I'm happy you found your own way to do this that was special and meaningful. Of course, I'd be lying if I told you that I wouldn't have accepted your proposal had you asked me the day I got back from North Carolina. None of the worries you had all along ever crossed my mind. It was a guaranteed yes, no matter how you did it. But this was magical, Gunner. I love you that much more for giving us something so special. Thank you."

He lifted our hands up and brought the back of mine to his mouth. After kissing me there, he whispered, "You're welcome, Sage."

From that point forward, I started looking at all the blessings that had come my way from the minute Gunner walked back into my life. That was going to be my focus. Anyone who had a problem with it would have to deal with it on their own because I wasn't going to change who I was for them.

Knowing that Marissa was proud of me only solidified my decision to continue to do what was best for me.

"Are you planning to tell the rest of the staff?" she finally asked.

"Yeah. Gunner and I are both excited about it, so I have no reason to hide it. We haven't told our parents yet, but we're planning to surprise them with it tomorrow morning," I said. "I'm relatively certain nobody here will be reaching out to them to spill the beans before we have the chance."

Marissa laughed.

Just then, Warren popped his head in the door and said, "Hey, Sage, we want you to take a look at these models we have. That storm we've been watching since late last week is looking like it's going to be pretty big tomorrow. We want to review the models with you before you're on."

"Okay, Warren. I'll be right there," I replied.

I looked back at Marissa and said, "And there is the official end to my vacation."

Marissa giggled as the both of us walked out and got ourselves to work.

Hours later, long after I'd first arrived back at work, I was ready to leave and head home to Gunner. After saying goodbye to my co-workers, I gathered up my things and pulled out my phone as I walked to the door.

"Hello?"

"Hey, handsome. I just wanted to let you know that I'm leaving work now," I greeted him.

"Okay. Do you want me to make you anything to eat for when you get here?" he asked.

I pushed open the door and stepped outside. As I walked down the steps and toward my car, I answered, "No. I ate my dinner already and brought a few extra snacks with me. Besides, I'm not sure where else I'd put any more food."

Gunner let out a chuckle and responded, "Okay. I'll see you in about ten minutes then. Be careful."

"I will. I love you."

"Love you, too."

I disconnected the call and was about to put my phone back in my purse when I saw a woman crouched down by the front passenger side tire of the van parked next to my vehicle.

"Did you get a flat?" I asked.

The woman looked up, seemingly startled by my presence, and stammered, "Oh, um, yeah. I, uh—"

"Can I call someone for you?" I offered. "Or, I work right inside. I'm sure one of the guys could come out and—"

I didn't get to finish asking my question because I was stunned into silence when the sliding door was flung open and a man jumped out. The woman pushed past me as he came toward me. I started taking steps backward, but he lunged forward and grabbed ahold of my arm. I twisted my neck in the opposite direction ready to call out to the woman for help when I noticed she had already rounded the vehicle and got in behind the steering wheel.

The man yanked me toward him. I struggled against him, but he was much stronger. My biggest concern was shielding my unborn baby, so when he lifted me up and all but tossed me into the van, my only thought was to cradle my stomach. I landed on my side in the backseat of the van.

Before I could even get myself upright, the woman yelled from the front seat, "Get her purse!"

My purse was yanked down my arm. Luckily, it was the one opposite of the one holding my phone.

The door slid along the tracks and slammed shut as the man opened the front passenger side door and got in. I'd barely just got to sitting upright when the woman stepped on the gas and flew out of the parking lot. I tried to open the door, but they must have switched on the child safety locks.

That's when things went from bad to worse.

Because I had been kidnapped, and my water broke two seconds after the van pulled out of the lot.

Gunner

I disconnected the call with Sage, slipped my phone into my back pocket, and bent to take the clothing out of the dryer. When we got back from our little trip last night, Sage refused to do any laundry. It didn't really much matter to me, but she wasn't one who liked having it pile up either. Given how great the weekend had been for the both of us, she insisted that it not end with laundry and that she'd do it today.

When I got home earlier tonight, I saw that she had gotten some of it done before she went to work. There was still a load in the dryer and a load that hadn't gone into the washing machine yet. I threw that load into the wash and went to make dinner. And just as I was making my way back to the laundry room to switch the clothing, I got the call from Sage.

After I removed the clothes from the dryer and put the clothes from the washer into the dryer, I carried the clean pile to our bedroom. I began folding and hanging everything and thought back on the day I'd had.

Of course, I knew that I had shared with Tyson that I was going to be proposing to Sage over the weekend, so when he and Trent walked into my office first thing this morning, I wasn't surprised.

"Well?" Tyson asked.

I grinned at him and confirmed, "She said yes."

My friends moved farther into my office and came over to shake my hand and congratulate me.

"Was she surprised?" Trent wondered.

Nodding, I confirmed, "She never knew it was coming. In fact, I could kick myself for not doing it sooner because she actually started thinking that I didn't want to get married to her."

"Oh, that's not good."

"Don't remind me," I started, rolling my eyes. "She told me I could have asked her when she came back from North Carolina and she would have said yes."

Both guys winced.

They knew how much I'd struggled to hold myself back from pushing for too much too soon with Sage. Knowing that it was really all for nothing wasn't an easy pill to swallow.

"Quinn's been dying to know about the ring," Tyson put in. "Did Sage like it?"

"Like isn't even the correct word to describe how she felt about the ring," I told him. "She loved it... said it was perfect."

"Good," he approved. "Quinn will be happy to hear it."

A moment later, Holden walked in. "What's going on in here? Discussing a new case?" he asked.

"We'll let Hayes fill you in," Tyson said.

Holden directed his attention to me, his face filled with concern, and I shared, "Sage and I got engaged over the weekend."

His eyes widened a moment before he moved toward me and pulled me toward him to give me a slap on the back. "Congratulations," he offered. "That's awesome news. Leni will be thrilled."

"I can't believe it," Trent declared.

"What?" I asked.

"All nine of us... down for the count," he explained.

We laughed because we couldn't deny it. Every single one of the Cunningham Security team members had fallen hard for the woman of their dreams. We'd all done it in a way that we could be considered down for the count. I knew there wasn't anything that any of us wouldn't do for our woman.

That was precisely the reason I was here now, folding and hanging up clothes. I didn't want Sage to come home after she had worked an arguably more physically demanding job today to have to worry about laundry. It had to be done. There was no law that said she had to be the only one to do it.

Just as I got the last shirt on a hanger, my phone rang.

When I pulled it out of my pocket and saw Sage's name on the display, I grew alert. With her being so close to the end of her pregnancy, I knew I could be getting that call at any moment.

I swiped my finger across the screen, but before I could say anything, all I heard was Sage screaming.

"Sage?" I called when the screaming stopped.

"Please take me to the hospital. I'm in labor," she cried out.

I was about to respond to tell her I was on my way when I heard someone in the background speak. "You're going somewhere to repent for your sins," a woman said.

My body froze.

"Momma doesn't like being ignored, especially by a sinner," a male voice chimed in.

What the hell was going on?

"Where are you taking me?" Sage asked. I could hear the fear and agony in her voice as I began moving through the house.

Please tell her. Please tell her, I chanted in my head.

"You'll see soon enough," the woman told her. "You need to be cleansed. My momma will make sure you repent for your sins. She's waiting for you behind the house."

"Your mom? Is she the one who's been posting all those comments online?" Sage pressed.

Good girl, Sage. Keep them talking. Lead me to you.

"So you did see them?" the man said. "She knew you were ignoring her on purpose."

I heard a bit of rustling before Sage spoke again. "My personal life isn't any of her business. You're all going to get into serious trouble for this. Please…" She paused and groaned. I wanted to climb through the phone to get to her. "Please, just take me to the hospital, and I'll let this go. I won't tell anyone."

She wouldn't. But I would.

I'd make it my life's mission to see to it that these sick people never walked free again if they brought any harm to Sage or our baby.

"Just five more minutes until we're—Bobby! She's got a phone!"

"What?" the man I now knew was Bobby returned.

"Gunner, please help me," Sage screamed, the terror in her voice something I knew I'd never forget for the rest of my life. "Summit Road up the side of Cedar Park Mountain."

"I'm coming, Sage," I assured her.

But the line went dead.

CHAPTER 19

Gunner

"HELLO?"

"Tyson, I need backup!" I barked into the phone as I sped away from the house toward the news station.

I just barely heard rustling around before he asked, "What's going on?"

"It's Sage. She was kidnapped."

After a brief pause, he questioned me. "Where are you?"

"Before our phone call was disconnected, she yelled out that they were on Summit Road going up the side of the Cedar Park Mountain," I informed him.

"I'm on my way," he assured me. "Do you know who has her?"

"Those people from social media who've been criticizing her the last few months," I answered. "She's in labor, Tyson."

"Shit," he bit out. "Any idea where they are taking her?"

Shaking my head even though he couldn't see me, I told him, "Not exactly. There was a man and a woman who both kept talking about their mother. They kept calling Sage a sinner and said their mother was going to make Sage repent for her sins somewhere behind the house. My woman begged them to take her to the hospital."

Silence stretched between us until Tyson finally declared, "I'm heading in the direction Sage said they were taking her. Keep your line clear in case she manages to get away and call you back. I'm getting Michaels on the line to see if we can track their location either based on her cell phone or from their social media."

"They've got her phone now," I warned him. "I tried to call her back after we got disconnected, but it didn't ring and went straight to voicemail."

"Okay. I'll have him start on social media," he decided. "We'll see if we can find an address for these people."

"I appreciate it, man," I told him, feeling desperate.

"We'll get her back safely," he promised.

At that, I ended the call. Tyson was going to get Trent, who was our resident computer genius, to locate Sage. As I pressed my foot down on the gas pedal just a bit more and continued to drive in the direction I believed they were heading, I hoped that when Trent called with an idea about where they were located I'd be close by.

All I could do was hope that Tyson was right, and we'd get Sage back safely. For weeks, I'd been so grateful that the extent of the terror I'd felt throughout my entire relationship with Sage was only in the beginning of it when she was in North Carolina. I thought I had lucked out. Apparently, I was wrong.

The Windsor landscape passed me by. Even though I could see that I was going faster than the speed limit, it felt like I was moving at a snail's pace.

I'd finally made it to Summit Road. When I'd gotten about halfway up the Cedar Park Mountain, my phone rang again.

"Did you find her?" I asked as my greeting when I glanced down and saw Trent's name on the display.

"I'm not sure, but I have an address to the house owned by Patricia Goodwin," he shared.

Patricia Goodwin was the name of the woman who'd been giving Sage grief for months online. Luckily, Sage stopped looking at the comments quite a while ago, which helped her emotional state a bit. While I understood that people had their opinions and would judge someone for their actions, I never thought someone would ever go this far over something like this. People had a right to their opinion. Sadly, some individuals thought that if you went against what they believed was right, they'd force you to see if from their perspective. In some cases, they didn't care who they hurt as they acted out their mission.

At that very moment, all I could think was that I was grateful we had someone like Trent on staff who could very quickly and very easily find someone's location with only a bit of information.

"Give me the address," I ordered.

Trent rattled off the address. I punched it into my GPS and saw that I was only seven minutes away.

"I'm going to get Tyson on this call now so we can get him the location, too," Trent advised.

A moment later, Tyson's voice came through the line. "What do you have, Michaels?" he asked.

Trent answered, "I've got you on a three-way call with Hayes right now. I've just given him the address to this woman's house."

He then gave Tyson the address.

"Okay, I'm eight minutes out," he declared.

"You're now two minutes behind me," I told him.

"I've just sent out texts to Locke and De Luca," Trent added. "They're coming, but they're probably fifteen minutes out."

I was happy to have the back up on the way, but I wasn't going to wait until they arrived to jump into action and save the woman I loved.

"So, what's behind this?" Tyson wondered.

Confused by his question, I asked, "What?"

"You told me that you heard them say something about taking Sage behind the house to have her repent for her sins. Something tells me they weren't talking about the backyard," he noted.

Fuck.

My mind had been so muddled I hadn't even considered that random fact. It suddenly crossed my mind that this is what it must have felt like for each of the guys on my team who'd experienced something similar when their woman was in trouble. It was like all of my logic and reasoning had gone out the window. And it was in this moment that I realized how lucky I was to work with this group of men. We'd not only all be there for one another whenever a situation arose related to work, but we'd also be guaranteed to have at least one guy with a clear head when someone on our team might not.

That's when I vaguely heard Trent hiss, "Fuck."

"What is it?" I asked, the sound of his voice snapping me back to reality.

"Maybe I'm wrong," he started. "But if these people have taken this too far because of their beliefs, I get the feeling they're going to take Sage to the Sunset Lake, which is located a few hundred feet from the back edge of their property."

"A lake? Why?" I asked.

Trent didn't respond.

A moment later, Tyson did.

"Baptism," he muttered.

"Cleansing her of what they view as her life of sin," Trent added.

"Damn it," I bit out. "It's early May. The temperature of a lake this high up in the mountains is still going to be freezing. She's in fucking labor!"

"Focus, Hayes," Trent instructed. "You could go to the address I gave you and walk around the back of the house. It looks like there's a clear path from there to the lake. Or you could turn left off of Summit Road onto a dirt road. It should be visible from the road you're on, even in the dark. That'll take you right to the lake."

"How far down that dirt road am I traveling?" I asked. "I've got to be nearly there by now."

"Five, maybe six hundred feet."

"Here it is, here it is," I said. "The road is narrow, but visible. Parking lights only when you come down it, Tyson. I don't want them getting spooked. I'm stopping before I get too close and will travel the rest on foot."

"I've got your back," Tyson promised.

"I'm disconnecting, guys. Michaels, I need you to call an ambulance," I ordered.

"I'm already on it," he assured me.

With that, I disconnected the call.

As badly as I wanted to speed down the road and get to Sage, I didn't want to risk alerting anyone to my presence. So, I crept slowly down it, stopped when I'd traveled about three hundred feet or so, and got out.

I moved as quickly and quietly as I could toward the lake. I saw a van in the distance, knew that it had to be them, and picked up my pace. As soon as I arrived at a clearing, my stomach sank.

Because I'd found Sage.

But she was lying on the ground, unconscious.

Sage
Eight minutes earlier

"Let's go," the woman ordered as I was hauled out of the back of the van.

I couldn't stand up straight, the cramping in my abdomen too much to bear.

"Please," I begged, doubled over in pain. "I'm in labor, and something isn't right. I need to get to the hospital."

"Momma will take care of you," the man said. "Momma will take care of you and the baby."

I had serious doubts about this woman's ability to 'take care of me' when she'd spent months posting negative comments and criticism about me and my life choices on the internet. Of course, I didn't share my feelings on that with her children. They seemed to be only slightly less crazy than I assumed she had to be if she'd set something like this up. Considering I thought her children were evil monsters, I could only imagine what I'd find when I finally had the privilege of meeting her.

At this point, I found myself wishing to be anywhere else. Heck, I would have rather been back in that hotel room in North Carolina with a hurricane raging outside the window. Anywhere but here.

As the man held on to my arm and dragged me beside him down a narrow dirt road, I silently prayed that Gunner had heard my desperate cries for help. I knew he would stop at nothing to find me; I just hoped he was able to locate me quickly enough based on the very little detail I shouted.

By the time we reached the edge of the dirt road, the vegetation had cleared. That's when I saw a woman, who could have only been Patricia from the internet, standing there with a dimly lit lantern in her hand.

"You made it," she said, her voice laced with a menacing tone.

"Yes, Momma, we did. We got her for you," her daughter confirmed.

Another painful contraction hit, and I couldn't stop myself from bending over and crying out in agony.

Somehow, I still didn't know what was worse, the pain or the terror I felt. I'd never experienced physical pain like this before. There was no doubt in my mind about that. But I wasn't sure I'd ever felt so scared before in all my life. And the fear I felt was magnified because it wasn't just my life on the line. I had my baby to think about, too.

"What's wrong with you?" Patricia asked.

The strength of the contraction was subsiding, so I jerked my arm out of her son's hold and shot back angrily, "My water broke, and I'm in labor. I'm not due for a few weeks yet. I need to get to a hospital."

Patricia's eyes widened in complete shock. Then, ever so slowly a devious grin broke out on her face. Seeing that terrified me more than I already had been.

"This is perfect," she declared.

"What do you want from me?" I questioned her.

Quite frankly, I didn't really care what she wanted. I just knew that the longer I had her talking to me, the more time Gunner would have to figure out where I was, and the less time she could bring any more harm to myself or the baby.

"We're going to give you a fresh start," she replied. "And we can make sure the baby gets the same absolution."

"Absolution?" I repeated. "What are you talking about?"

Patricia's eyes drifted away from me to the side where she jerked her chin. I looked in the direction she'd turned her attention, saw where she was indicating, and returned my stare to her. Once she focused her gaze on me again, she answered, "Forgiveness for your sins. We're going to absolve you and the baby tonight with a baptism. Then we'll show you the right way to lead your life."

I hadn't ever given birth before, but if this woman thought I was going to willingly deliver my child into the arms of a psychopath, she was going to be seriously disappointed. Looking around, I tried to figure out where I could go to get away, but I wasn't sure there was a way for me to do that. I was in labor at the top of a mountain in the dark where it was freezing cold and I had no idea where the closest hospital was.

It was then my body began trembling. Once again, I was left trying to figure out if this was a physical or emotional response. On one hand, I was still wearing my dress and heels from work. Thankfully, I'd put on my wool coat before I left the station, but it was doing little to help combat the frigid temperatures, especially considering how long I'd been outside. From an emotional standpoint, the fear I felt about what was going to happen to me and this baby if Gunner didn't find us soon was more than I could stand. I wouldn't have been surprised if that was the sole reason why I couldn't stop my body from shaking.

"Why are you doing this?" I asked. "Why is it any of your business what I do with my life? If I go to Hell for the choices I make, isn't that my cross to bear?"

"We're all here to do His work," Patricia informed me.

"And you think that kidnapping a pregnant woman who's

in labor after posting harassing and negative comments about her for months is the work God has sent you to do?" I scoffed.

I wasn't sure if she answered me because just then another contraction ripped through me. The pain was so unbearable, everything else ceased to exist.

Even the sound of my own screams.

In the next moment, something started happening to me. The pain never ceased. It just continued coming at me like a freight train.

Before I could stop it from happening, I felt my legs give out from underneath me. Patricia's son was still standing beside me. I leaned in his direction as I went down to the ground, hoping he would be decent enough to catch me before I fell and did any unnecessary harm to my baby who I had a feeling was already in trouble.

That was the last thing I remembered before my eyes rolled back in my head and I passed out.

CHAPTER 20

Gunner

SAGE WAS LYING LIFELESS ON THE GROUND.

I didn't know how that was possible when she told me she was in labor. Something had to be wrong.

Knowing that not only was Sage in serious trouble, but that our baby probably was too sparked a fire inside me. Months ago, I made a promise to Sage when she first told me she was pregnant that I was going to be there for her and this baby in every way that mattered. Days ago, I solidified my intent to keep my promise when I asked Sage to marry me. If I failed to deliver on that promise now, I didn't deserve either one of them.

Just as I was about to charge forward, I felt a hand on my shoulder and Tyson whisper, "What's happening?"

"Sage is unconscious," I told him, barely able to take my eyes off her.

"How many of them are there?" he asked.

"I think it's just the two kids and the mother," I whispered back. "I don't know if there are weapons, but I don't really care at this point. I've got to get to her."

Lorenzo De Luca, one of our co-workers, materialized a moment later. I didn't know how he had gotten here so fast, and I didn't really care. There were three of us and three of them.

As if sensing my urgency, Lorenzo noted, "Locke is coming right behind me. You go to Sage; Tyson and I will cover you."

I dipped my chin and took off. As I emerged from the dark shadows with Tyson and Lorenzo right behind me, I vaguely heard the mother who was standing over Sage tell her son, "We need to get her in the wa—"

I didn't look up. I trusted Tyson and Lorenzo to do what they said they were going to do. They'd cover me while I went to Sage. Kneeling down beside her, I checked for a pulse. I found it, felt a smidge of relief, and called, "Sage."

There was no response.

I shook her shoulders and repeated, "Sage."

Out of sheer instinct, my hand went to her belly. It was hard. My only guess was that she was having a contraction.

"Sage, are you with me?" I called again.

There was a slight groan, and that noise was like music to my ears.

"That's it, babe. Come back to me," I encouraged her.

I could just barely make out Sage's eyes fluttering open. As soon as she saw me, her eyes widened, she gripped my hand, and cried, "The baby is coming. Something is wrong."

Fuck.

Fuck!

"Can I pick you up?" I asked, wanting to get her off the cold ground and back into the warmth of my car.

Her chest was rising and falling rapidly. "The baby... the baby is..."

That was all she got out before she screamed in pain.

It suddenly dawned on me. "Is the baby coming now?" I asked.

Her fingers had curled into the palm of my hand and were digging in hard. "Yes!" she panted.

"I've got a flashlight and a blanket in my car," Holden declared before taking off.

Apparently, I'd been so focused on Sage, I hadn't realized he'd arrived. Not only that, he was able to assess the situation with her because Tyson and Lorenzo had neutralized the three suspects.

Realizing how dire the situation was, I tried to remain calm. "I'm going to take your shoes and nylons off," I told Sage. "I need to see what's happening, okay?"

"Please, Gunner," she begged. "Please help me."

"I've got you, honey," I assured her as I yanked off her shoes and slipped my hands underneath her dress so I could remove her stockings and panties.

"Flashlight," Holden announced.

I glanced up and took it out of his hand as he draped the blanket over Sage's thighs and abdomen.

I set the flashlight down on the ground between Sage's legs and saw our baby's head.

"Shit," I hissed quietly. Not wanting to alarm Sage, I confirmed what she already knew, "The baby is coming."

"I have to push," she exclaimed.

I did not want her to push. I wanted the paramedics to arrive first. I looked up at Holden, and I'm certain he saw the terror in my eyes. He positioned himself by Sage's head and dipped his chin. That's when I encouraged her. "Okay, then push."

"If you need to hold on to something, you've got me," Holden offered.

Not even thirty seconds later, through Sage's cries and pushes, I witnessed a miracle. My child's head was there.

"The head is out, Sage," I told her. "Good job, honey."

Sadly, the excitement I felt was short-lived because when I looked back down, I saw that there was a cord wrapped around the baby's neck.

I tried to remove the cord immediately, but Sage started to push again. The cord grew tighter as she did.

"Stop pushing," I instructed. "Stop pushing."

"Gunner," Sage whimpered.

"The cord is around the baby's neck," I explained. Instantly, Sage stopped pushing, and I knew I likely didn't have much time. I tried to slip my finger under the cord, desperately trying to free it. It took a few tries, but I eventually managed to slip it over the baby's head.

"Okay, Sage, you can push again," I told her as I looked up at her.

She looked utterly exhausted, but she used one hand to grab behind her thigh while the other curled around Holden's hand. Holden used his free hand to help support Sage behind her head as she pushed.

It felt like hours had passed, but I knew it hadn't been more than a few seconds when the shoulders popped out and the baby slid effortlessly the rest of the way out. Turning the baby over, I saw that I'd just delivered my daughter.

"It's a girl," I told Sage as I placed the baby on her belly.

In the distance, I heard the faint sound of sirens.

"Why isn't she crying?" Sage worried.

My eyes flew from Sage's back to my daughter. Holden pulled out his phone, switched on the light, and held it up over us. That's when I noticed my little girl was blue.

"Fuck," I hissed, panic gripping every inch of me.

I started stroking along her back. "Come on, baby girl," I whispered. Her lifeless body only moved with each movement of my hand on her.

"Gunner," Sage called, her worry growing by the second. "Please save our daughter."

The sound of the sirens drew nearer as fear invaded every cell of my body. Moments later, a tiny cry filled the air around us. There was no way to describe the immense feeling of relief I felt hearing her cry.

"Good girl," I praised her. The husky tone of my voice, I'm certain, giving away just how emotional a moment it had been for me.

"Handsome."

I looked up into Sage's eyes. They were filled with tears. Despite the emotions she was feeling, she managed to push past them and rasped, "She's beautiful."

Nodding, I agreed, "She is, baby. You did so good."

Sage reached out and touched my arm. "Give her a good name… something unique," she begged. There was an edge of desperation in her tone.

"Sage?" I called, not liking the sound of her voice.

"Give her the world," she said softly.

I didn't know why Sage was talking to me like she wasn't going to be around to do any of this herself.

Before I could say anything, she breathed, "Make sure she knows how much I love her… how much I love both of you."

No sooner did she get those words out when she closed her eyes. "Sage!" I shouted.

She didn't respond.

"She's hemorrhaging," someone yelled out.

I'd been so caught up in what Sage had been saying to me that I hadn't noticed the paramedics arrived. The police had as well. In the moments that followed, people were swirling around me. I couldn't pay any attention to anything, though.

My eyes remained glued to Sage. This couldn't be happening.

We couldn't have come this far only to have this happen. Sage needed to wake up. Her daughter needed her. *I* needed her.

"There's no pulse," one of the medics declared.

No.

No. No. *No!*

"Sage," I whispered.

"Sir?" a paramedic broke into my thoughts.

I didn't take my eyes off the love of my life.

"Sir, we need you to step back so we can help her."

The next thing I knew, I felt a hand on my shoulder as Holden urged, "Come on, let's move back."

I shook my head. I couldn't. I couldn't walk away from her even though I knew that was the only way to save her.

Thankfully, my friends were there to do for me what I couldn't. Tyson had materialized beside me and helped Holden lift me from the ground and away from Sage's body. Away from my baby.

"Sage!!" I yelled.

"Come on, brother," Tyson urged, moving me backward.

I struggled against Tyson and Holden, wanting… no, needing to be by my girls.

"Sage!" I shouted.

Nothing. There was nothing from her.

"Let them help her," Holden encouraged me.

"She's got to wake up," I insisted, the ragged edge of my voice indicating I was close to breaking.

"She's going to wake up," Tyson assured me.

He didn't know that. He couldn't make that promise to me.

But I was so desperate to cling to any hope there was that I believed him anyway.

I felt numb.

Thinking back to when I was a kid living with a single mom who was struggling to make ends meet, I thought that was the worst of it. I thought I'd paid my dues at a young age and would experience a life of bounty as long as I worked hard enough.

I had it. It was right there in my grasp, and somehow, mere hours ago it all started slipping away.

Was I going to become my mom?

No, I wouldn't. I'd be far worse off.

My mother pushed forward every day despite the fact that my father left us.

I'd be a single father, struggling to raise his daughter because he couldn't move forward. The gaping hole in my heart would be there forever, only growing larger and larger as each day went by without Sage.

I knew I wouldn't survive it.

Seeing Sage lying on the cold ground by that lake as the life left her body and again as I rode in the ambulance with our daughter in my arms, I wondered how it was possible to have the best day of your life also be the worst.

When we arrived at the hospital, my little girl was whisked out of my arms and taken to be assessed. I was ushered into a private waiting room. And Sage was taken somewhere. I didn't know where she was, what was happening to her, or if she'd ever come back to me.

I had no concept of time; it felt like it was crawling by. But the clock indicated that it was roughly thirty minutes after

I'd been put in the waiting room when the door opened and Tyson walked in.

"Any word on Sage?" he asked.

I looked up from where I had my hands clasped in front of me, my elbows resting on my thighs. I shook my head and felt a wave of disappointment and despair flood me.

"What about the baby?" he pressed.

"They took her from me the minute we got here," I started. "I held her in my arms the whole way here. She seemed okay, but she's a preemie. I hope they're just being extra cautious."

The silence stretched between us. I didn't mind that. In fact, I appreciated Tyson's silent support while it lasted. Eventually, because he was a good friend, he asked, "Have you called your parents?"

I nodded. "Yeah."

That was the only thing I'd managed to do. My mom and Simon were on their way. Mike and Rose were checking flights. They had originally planned to come out in two weeks to be here for the baby's arrival. Obviously, things had changed.

"That's good," he started. "Dom and Cruz rode together and met us up that mountain. I gave Cruz your keys, so he's going to bring your truck here."

As if on cue, the door opened and Cruz walked in followed by the rest of my co-workers: Holden, Dom, Lorenzo, Trent, Levi, and Pierce.

Seeing them all there should have made me feel good. It did. But it also made me realize that these guys knew just how serious this was, especially when I took in all their faces.

Grim and solemn while remaining benevolent and empathetic.

It was too much for me to take. I dropped my gaze to the floor, clenched my jaw, and pressed the base of my palms into my eye sockets.

I didn't have to look up to know the guys had filled the seats and bare walls around me. That's what family did. They'd be there to support you and lift you up when you were facing the worst. Sadly, I wasn't sure that even they would be able to help me if Sage didn't survive.

Time passed excruciatingly slow.

I heard the occasional phone call come through. There were murmured conversations around the room. But mostly, it remained silent.

At least, it was until I spoke.

"There was so much blood in that ambulance," I declared, my voice husky.

Tyson's hand came to my shoulder and squeezed. I closed my eyes and recalled the terrifying scene. I was no doctor, but I didn't see how it was possible for someone to lose as much blood as Sage did and still survive.

"She's going to pull through," Trent insisted.

Shaking my head, I lifted my gaze and stated, "You didn't see it. I've never seen that much blood in my life."

"Sage is a mom now," Lorenzo chimed in. "She's got someone depending on her to pull through."

"I called Kendall on my way here," Dom shared. "She said she'll check on the baby and come update you personally as soon as she has any news."

Kendall was one of Dom's sisters. She was also a nurse in the maternity ward here at the hospital.

I nodded in acknowledgment. "I appreciate that."

A minute later, I was shaking my head back and forth.

"What is it, man?" Tyson asked.

I twisted my neck and looked directly at him. "How am I going to raise a little girl on my own?" I asked.

"You won't," Holden promised.

He was genuinely convinced that was the truth. I just didn't know if he felt that way because he believed Sage would pull through and be there with me, or if he just knew that I had too many people in my life that I'd never be alone.

Just then, the door opened again. My eyes shot to it, and I saw Kendall walking in.

Immediately, I stood. I couldn't read the look on her face. As she approached me, I stopped breathing. The tension in the room was palpable.

Please tell me my baby girl is okay, I thought.

Kendall stopped inches in front of me, kept her eyes locked on mine for what felt like hours, before she threw her arms around my neck, and burst out with, "Congratulations, Gunner. Your daughter is absolutely perfect."

Relief swept through me. All I could do was wrap my arms around Kendall and hold on tight. "Thank you," I whispered.

When I finally let Kendall go, she took a step back and added, "She's teeny, but she's going to be fine."

"What about Sage? Do you know anything about her?" I asked.

Kendall shook her head. "I'm sorry, I don't."

I took in a deep breath as I gave her a nod. I didn't get a chance to say anything else because the door opened again. This time, I didn't recognize the person who entered other than to know it was the doctor.

He looked around the room and said, "I'm looking for Gunner Hayes."

"That's me, sir," I declared, taking a step forward.

He extended his hand to me and introduced himself. "I'm Dr. Roberts. I've got someone who wants to see you," he said.

Hope surged in my chest. "Sage?" I asked.

He smiled and dipped his chin. There was a collective sigh of relief in the room. "The moment we revived her, she asked for you."

"Please take me to her," I demanded.

Without hesitating, he turned and moved to the door.

Kendall stepped in front of me and explained, "I'll check on Sage's status. If all is good, I'll sneak a little visitor into the room for the both of you."

"I'd appreciate that. Thanks, Kendall."

Before I walked out, I turned back to look at the guys. I didn't get a chance to say anything because Levi spoke before I could.

"We know, Gunner. Just go to your girls," he ordered.

I dipped my chin and walked out.

I'm not sure what my expectations were when I walked into Sage's room. All I knew was that I wanted physical proof that she was alive and well.

On the way to Sage's room, the doctor had filled me in on what happened, but I found it difficult to really pay attention. The only thing I caught him saying was that Dr. Perry had been tied up performing a cesarean section on another patient, so he was unavailable to help with Sage. Truthfully, it didn't matter, though. Once he'd confirmed that she'd woken up and asked for me, nothing else really mattered. I knew that after I had some time to process everything that had happened, I'd talk to the doctor again. I just needed to do that when I had a clear head.

"And here she is," he declared, stopping in front of a room.

"Thanks, doctor."

He nodded and said, "I'll be back around later to check on her."

I opened the door and walked into Sage's room. When I stepped around the curtain, I saw her there in the bed, looking pale and exhausted. Never had I seen a more beautiful sight in my life.

When her eyes met mine, she asked, "Did you give her a name?"

I don't know what came over me, but I had a feeling it was a mix of everything I'd felt since the moment I got that call from Sage after she'd been kidnapped. Whatever it was propelled me forward until I was at the side of her bed. I bent at the waist, cupped her opposite cheek in my hand, and kissed the one closest to me. Then I was like a baby. Fully grown, crying my eyes out with my face buried in her neck as I sat on the edge of her bed.

"Gunner..." She trailed off, her voice a touch over a whisper. I could feel one of her hands stroking up and down my back as the other came up to the back of my head.

She was touching me.

Mere minutes ago, I was certain that I was never going to experience the privilege of having her touch me ever again. I didn't think I'd ever be able to put my hands on her or kiss her. I wholeheartedly believed I'd lost her.

At some point, I managed to pull back and look at her beautiful face again.

After giving myself some time to allow it to sink in that she was here talking to me, I admitted, "I was so scared tonight, Sage. Seeing you like that was the worst thing I've ever experienced."

Sage squeezed my arm. "I'm sorry you went through that," she lamented.

"It wasn't your fault," I assured her.

She gave me a small smile and asked, "How is our little girl?"

I felt my whole body light up just thinking about her beautiful little face. "She's good," I started. "Dom's sister, Kendall, is a nurse here. She came down and told me that our daughter is perfect. Kendall said she was going to get her and bring her to your room."

Just then, there was a knock on the door. I turned as it opened and heard Kendall declare, "I've got a visitor."

She came around the curtain with a big smile on her face as she pushed the cart with our girl inside. Without hesitating, she lifted my baby in her arms and asked, "Does Mommy want her or does Daddy?"

I looked at Sage. "Her mom hasn't held her yet," I answered.

Kendall moved closer to the bed and placed my daughter in Sage's arms. The minute she held her, Sage's eyes filled with tears. She looked up at Kendall and asked, "Is she okay? She's so tiny."

Kendall nodded. "Yes, she's good. Passed all her tests, too. The only thing we really need to do now is talk about feeding. If you're planning to breastfeed, we'd want to try to get her to latch on now. It's a little bit past the point at which we'd want to get that done."

"Yes, I'd like to try," Sage insisted.

"Would you like me to help you the first time?" Kendall offered.

"If you don't mind," Sage replied.

Kendall shook her head. "Not at all."

For the next ten minutes or so, Kendall talked to Sage about breastfeeding and helped her with getting our baby latched on for the first time. Once Sage was comfortable, Kendall asked, "Now, did you want to keep her in the room with you, or did you want us to take care of her in the nursery?"

Sage looked at me before returning her attention to Kendall. "I'd like to keep her here with me as long as that's alright," she decided.

"Absolutely. I'll come back in later to check on everyone, but if you need anything in the meantime, don't hesitate to hit your call button."

"Thank you," Sage and I replied in unison.

"You're welcome. And congratulations again."

With that, Kendall left the room and we were alone again. I took a moment to just watch as Sage nursed our girl. This was my family. My girls. There was no better feeling.

I sat back down on the bed beside Sage and stroked the back of my finger along my daughter's cheek. Her skin was so soft. She was the sweetest little thing I'd ever seen.

"So?" Sage asked, interrupting my adoration of the tiny girl in her arms.

I looked up at her and asked, "So what?"

"You never answered me before," she started. "Did you give her a name?"

I swallowed hard, wondering if the name I'd been thinking about would be something Sage would like.

"Well, I was thinking we could call her Ivy," I shared.

"Ivy?" Sage repeated. "Where did that name come from?"

Nodding, I explained, "Well, it's a botanical name like

your own. But it also symbolizes eternity. For me, especially after a night like tonight, the idea that she'll be around forever and that she'll bond us for the rest of our lives is one that I really like."

Sage didn't respond. She simply held my eyes for a very long time. I started to think that perhaps she didn't like the name and she just didn't know how to tell me. Not wanting her to have to agree to something that didn't sit well with her, I stressed, "If you don't like it or you had something else in mind, we don't have to use Ivy. Honestly, Sage, whatever you want to name her is going to be fine with me."

"Ivy Steele Hayes," she stated.

"What?"

"Ivy Steele Hayes," she repeated. She looked down at our daughter and went on, "If she's going to have a name that reminds you of me and our relationship, I need her to have a name that reminds me of you. So, it's Steele. Because I have no doubt that she's going to be strong just like her daddy."

Ivy Steele Hayes.

My firstborn.

My daughter.

"I love you, Sage," I proclaimed.

After she lifted her gaze to mine, she returned, "I love you, too, Gunner."

EPILOGUE

Sage
Five Months Later

"Are you on your way?"

"I just got in my truck," Gunner replied. "I'm heading home."

"Perfect. Ivy and I have a surprise for you when you get here," I told him.

Gunner let out a laugh before he teased, "Coming from you that could mean good or bad things for me. Given my little lady is in on it, I'm going to hope she talked you out of anything too crazy."

"Ha. Ha. You're so funny. We'll see you soon."

"Love you."

"Love you, too."

I pulled my phone from my ear and looked down at my daughter. "Mommy's not crazy, right?" I asked her.

Ivy grinned at me. Quite frankly, I wasn't sure she would have grinned if she could see the get-up I had her in at the moment. Of course, that was the norm for her. She was the happiest baby in the world.

It was almost surreal to think that there had been a very real possibility that one or both of us might not have been here if things had gone different for us a few months ago.

As it turned out, I had suffered a placental abruption when I went into labor. In a controlled environment, a placental abruption is a scary and risky business. The situation I'd been in should have been fatal for both Ivy and me.

Luckily, Gunner and his team of co-workers were the best at what they did, and they managed to find me before things went to a place that we couldn't come back from. I almost didn't. I'd lost a lot of blood and needed to be transfused by the time they got me to the hospital. The doctors kept me in the hospital an extra couple days just as a precautionary measure, and I was fortunate to not experience any further complications.

Dr. Perry had been concerned about the reason I had the placental abruption in the first place. There hadn't been anything through the length of my pregnancy that indicated it would happen. And while there didn't necessarily have to be, Gunner and I were a bit alarmed.

Even though we'd been through a lot and weren't anywhere near ready to have another baby, we knew we wanted more than one. That said, Gunner wanted to know what the chances were that this could happen again.

After filling him in on the events of the night I went into labor and gave birth to Ivy, Dr. Perry said it was possible for the placental abruption to occur if there is trauma to the abdomen. The best I could come up with was that it might have happened when I'd struggled and was then tossed into the back of the van.

Ultimately, Dr. Perry saw no reason for Gunner and me to stop ourselves from having another baby when we felt we were ready.

Ever since Ivy and I were discharged from the hospital and sent home, life had been wonderful. I loved being a mother. More than that, I loved being a mother to Ivy alongside her father.

Gunner was the world's best dad. For the first few weeks, he stayed home from work to be with us. He was just as involved in taking care of Ivy as I was. If she woke up in the middle of the night, he'd get up with her. He'd changed diapers or bring her to me for her feedings.

The two of us didn't really have any clue if we were doing everything right all the time, but we were having a great time learning as we went along.

Ivy was such a pleasant baby, too, so she made it easy. Of course, Gunner and I still suffered from sleepless nights and exhaustion, but we didn't complain. She was our greatest joy, and we could hardly imagine our lives without her.

Sometimes, I would think back to what happened the night she was born, and I'd remember her not breathing. I'd struggled for a while not to let my anger consume me at times. But once Patricia and her two children were charged and sentenced, I found a way to let it go and move on.

Work was another thing.

The truth was that I was dealing with a mix of emotions about returning to work. If I was being completely honest, the fact that the last time I'd left work resulted in me being kidnapped made it a little intimidating to want to return. Ultimately, though, I knew what happened was a freak thing, and it wasn't likely that something like that would ever happen again.

But beyond that, I truly adored being a mother. Ivy was my whole world. There was a small part of me that always had the thought in the back of my mind how close we'd been to losing her. It made me not want to ever miss a single moment of her life, very much the same way Gunner didn't want to miss a single moment of my pregnancy.

So, I sat down with Gunner about a month before I was scheduled to return to work. Ivy was just two months old at the time.

"I don't want to leave her," I said.

"What do you mean? Where are you going?" he asked.

"Next month," I clarified. "I've been thinking a lot about it, and I really don't want to go back to work just yet."

There wasn't an ounce of hesitation as Gunner replied, "So stay home with her."

I was genuinely surprised by his immediate support. "Really? Just like that? You make it sound so simple."

He cocked an eyebrow and countered, "I'm making it sound simple because it is simple. We sold my condo a while ago, took all the money, and paid off this place. We're fine. Would you rather have me fight you on it and tell you that you need to go back to work next month when the truth is that you don't?"

I swallowed hard, loving that I was hearing everything I would have hoped for while wondering what I'd done to deserve it.

"Of course not," I rasped. "I just… I didn't want to make any assumptions. And I don't want you to think that it's your sole responsibility to provide for us. I'm sure I'll go back eventually, but I'm just not ready for it yet."

"Sage, babe, I know you don't expect that of me, but I'm honored to have the responsibility. You should at least know how much that would mean to me. To know that I can give my child the things I didn't have—food in her belly and her mama's belly, a roof over both of their heads, and a home with two loving parents—is all I've ever wanted. This doesn't feel like a chore."

Gunner had always been such a sweet man, so I don't know why I ever expected the conversation would have gone any differently than it did. But for whatever reason, after he'd delivered all of that, I couldn't stop myself from bursting into tears. As he always did, Gunner comforted me while I blamed it all on the fact that my hormones hadn't quite returned to normal. Because he was such a gentleman, Gunner never called me out on it either.

Now, I'd been home with Ivy since the day we were discharged from the hospital, and it was the most rewarding experience of my life. I loved watching her grow and being able to witness her hit all the different milestones. Every day was a new adventure. Sometimes the days were filled with visits from Ivy's grandparents while other days were just the two of us hanging out with each other.

Today was one of those days.

Just then, I glanced out the window and saw Gunner's truck pull into the driveway.

"Daddy's home, Ivy!" I bubbled with excitement. "Just wait until he sees you."

My little girl grinned at me.

Several moments later, the door opened. I waited patiently for Gunner to enter the living room so he could see what I'd done.

The next thing I knew, I was struggling not to burst into a fit of laughter.

Gunner walked in, took one look at us, and stopped dead in his tracks. He tipped his head to the side, gave Ivy a sympathetic look, and pinned his gaze on me.

"What did you do to our daughter?" he asked.

"She looks adorable!" I cried.

Gunner didn't reply. He stood there a moment staring at his baby. His face softened at the sight of her pudgy cheeks, and he moved toward us.

Taking her out of my arms, he lifted her up, kissed her cheek, and asked, "What did Mama do to you, sweet pea?"

Ivy clapped her hands on her daddy's face as a stream of drool fell from her mouth. Gunner held her to his chest, looked at me, and said, "You dressed her up as a peacock."

"Isn't it great?" I bubbled, shifting my attention from Gunner to Ivy.

It was a few days before Halloween, and I finally had a chance to try on the costume I'd ordered for Ivy's first big holiday.

I felt like I'd been waiting for this moment for the last year. Gunner had revived my love of the holidays, and Ivy's first year of them was going to be a big deal.

"Her face is the only thing visible in this contraption," he noted.

I beamed at him and replied, "I know. She's got the best set of baby cheeks in town, so it's perfect for her."

Gunner shook his head at me in disbelief before turning his attention to Ivy and giving her another kiss. Then he murmured quietly, "I'm sorry about this, sweet pea. When you're older, I hope you'll know how badly I wanted to try and save you from this."

I narrowed my eyes at him just as he brought his gaze to me and continued, "But nothing makes me happier than seeing your mom as joyful as she is when she's excited about something for you; so unfortunately, you're stuck looking like a peacock this Halloween."

Taking a step forward, I held my arms out and took Ivy

from Gunner. "She's the most adorable peacock there ever was," I started. "Which is why you need to run upstairs and change your clothes. I put a shirt out on the bed for you."

Gunner's brows pulled together. "What exactly am I getting changed for? Where are we going?" he wondered.

"Pictures!" I declared.

"Pictures?" he repeated.

I dipped my chin. "Pictures. This is Ivy's first Halloween. We're taking family photos. I've set everything up outside."

Gunner went from confused to surprised. "You have something set up outside?" he asked.

Nodding, I explained, "Ivy and I have been busy girls. We went out shopping and got all of our props and a few extra decorations a few days ago. Today, we set everything up after you left for work this morning. And if you don't hurry, we're not going to be able to get these pictures done because there's not a lot of daylight left."

After a moment of hesitation, Gunner leaned forward, gave me a kiss, and said, "I'll be right back."

"Thanks, handsome," I called as he walked away.

Even though Gunner might have thought that my ideas were crazy or that I'd picked out the most ridiculous costume for our daughter, he didn't hesitate to give me what I wanted. He wasted no time. No sooner had he left to get himself changed when he returned.

I took him outside, showed him what I'd worked on earlier in the day, and immediately got Ivy positioned. After directing Gunner to his position, I set up the camera I'd purchased almost immediately after Ivy and I got home from the hospital.

From there, I set a timer and hurried over to my family. We waited for the click before I went back, checked the image, and asked Gunner to do just one more. After the second family photo was taken, I ended up taking a couple of shots of just Ivy or Ivy with her dad. Gunner insisted on switching out with me at one point, claiming that there were enough pictures of Ivy and him together all over our house but not nearly enough of me with her.

We switched and Gunner got behind the lens. When he felt he'd take a sufficient amount of photos, we went inside to have dinner. While I fed Ivy, Gunner took the dinner I had already prepped and popped it in the oven.

And for the rest of the evening, we spent time together catching up on our days and playing with Ivy.

That night, after our daughter was asleep in her crib, Gunner had made love to me, and as we were cuddling, I blurted, "What do you think about September twentieth."

"What?"

"For our wedding," I began. "I've been thinking about it a lot more over the past few weeks and that's the date I like."

"Sage, it doesn't matter to me when we do it. If you want September twentieth, we can do that," he assured me. "Is there a reason you picked that day?"

"Yeah. It was the day, just over a year ago, that you walked back into my life after all those years. It was the day we conceived Ivy. I think it should be the day we start our married life together."

Gunner, who was spooning me, pressed his lips to the skin at the side of my throat as his arm tightened around me. His mouth moved to my ear where he whispered, "September twentieth it is."

"I don't need anything big or fancy," I told him. "I just want our parents and our close friends. Is that okay with you?"

"Sage?"

"Yeah?"

"My only goal in life is to give you the whole world," he started. "No matter what you want, I'll do what I can to give it to you. Big wedding or small, I don't care. I want you. And Ivy. And any more babies we decide to bring into this world. You can choose how we celebrate all of it."

The fingers of my hand that had been resting on the top of Gunner's pressed in. "How soon do you want another baby?" I wondered.

"Whenever you're ready to put your body through it again," he replied.

Silence stretched between us while I considered the possibility of another pregnancy. Eventually, I shared, "Let's wait until Ivy is at least a year old. Then we can start trying."

"You'll be okay with being pregnant again before we get married?" he asked.

"Are you planning to leave me?" I retorted, a small laugh escaping.

"Not at all."

"Then yes, Gunner. I'm okay with being pregnant again before we get married. It's not going to change the way we feel about one another, so whenever it happens is fine with me. I just want to give Ivy a bit more time with the two of us before we do that."

The silence fell between us again. This time, it was Gunner who broke it.

"You are the best decision I ever made, Sage," he said softly.

"I feel the same way."

"I love you," he added.

"I love you, too."

With that, Gunner kissed my neck again before giving me another squeeze. Moments later, we drifted.

And I did it feeling grateful that my life had led me to this very moment with this incredible man.

BONUS EPILOGUE

Gunner

"**D**ADDY, DO YOU HAVE MY BOARDS READY?"

My neck twisted and I looked down at the face of the little girl whose voice had asked the question.

"Sweet pea, you ask me that every time we go riding. Have I ever not had your boards ready?" I returned.

"I'm just making sure," Ivy said. "I want to bring all of them because I've got to practice for the contest."

Nodding, I assured her, "I know. I've got everything ready to go for you and Hunter. Speaking of which, where is your brother?"

"Mom's helping him get his gear on," Ivy replied.

I dipped my chin. "Okay. We're heading out as soon as Mom and Hunter are ready, so make sure you grab a snack before we go."

"Okay."

At my instructions, my daughter turned and walked away toward the kitchen. As I returned my attention to the gear bag, confirming we had everything we needed, I couldn't help but let out a laugh.

Ivy was eight now.

Eight.

My sweet little girl was growing faster than I was prepared for. And it seemed that once her brother arrived, time started moving even faster.

Hunter was six years old, and while I believed I'd always be concerned about Ivy because she was my daughter, I was convinced Hunter would be the reason I ended up going gray early. My son was a terror. It wasn't necessarily in a bad way; Hunter had a drive that reminded me a lot of how I'd been when I was a kid.

I knew that could be a good thing in a lot of areas; I just wondered how he'd use that drive the older he got.

Overall, my kids growing up so quickly was more than I could handle. So, I didn't. I just did my best to ignore the fact that the days were long and the years were short and tried to focus on what was happening now.

Like today.

It was late January, and we were heading to Parks Ridge Ski Resort in Windsor's neighboring city of Rising Sun to snowboard. Parks Ridge was the home mountain to several professional snowboarders. My boss' brother was one of those snowboarders.

And it seemed that my kids had plans to become professional riders as well.

The winter before Ivy turned four, I held true to my word to Sage and started teaching my daughter how to snowboard.

Ivy was a natural. She picked it up very quickly.

I had done the same with Hunter when he was three. And he was just like his sister.

Seeing my kids riding filled me with a level of pride I couldn't even begin to describe. I never realized how much of an effect it would have on me, and it was all thanks to my wife that I even got to experience it. Had Sage not insisted on me promising her that

I'd teach our children how to ride, I wasn't sure it was something I'd have ever returned to unless they specifically asked to try it.

By the time that happened, if at all, so much valuable time would have been wasted.

Now, they were well on their way to fulfilling their dreams. Because in just two weeks, both Ivy and Hunter were going to be competing in a contest being hosted by Blackman Boards at Parks Ridge. They were both going to be competing in the banked slalom course. Ivy had recently started riding the halfpipe and was going to compete in that as well. Hunter was going to be doing jumps.

I couldn't have been prouder of my kids.

And I was just as proud of my wife.

While Sage had no plans to ever compete nor had she ever gone snowboarding before, she came out with us every single time. She didn't care that our children picked up the sport faster than she did. She loved being there with them and watching them succeed.

Once I was confident in their abilities, I found myself spending more time trying to teach her how to be a better rider. And over the last year, Sage had improved tremendously.

As though she knew I was thinking about her, my gorgeous wife entered the room as she called out to Hunter, "Grab yourself a snack because we're leaving in five minutes."

"Okay, Mom!" he yelled back.

I'd just finished going through the gear bag and had zipped it up as Sage moved in my direction. By the time she made it to where I was, I stood.

"Hey, stranger," I said softly as I slipped my arm around her waist and gave her a kiss.

"It's been close to ten years, handsome," Sage started. "I'm not exactly a stranger anymore."

I grinned and assured her, "Calling you a stranger isn't a bad thing. To this very day, after all these years, you still manage to surprise me, Sage."

That was the truth. I still had days that I marveled over the woman standing in my arms. Nearly every day, Sage gave me something special. Just when I thought I had her all figured out, she'd show me a different side to her. Those different sides were always changing, too. And it was never just in one area of our lives.

Seeing her with Ivy, I thought I knew the kind of mother she was. But then we had Hunter, and I realized she had a completely different approach to raising our son. Sage was the best kind of mother. She gave her time freely to our children and was honored to do it. She didn't complain about the messes they made, the dirty laundry that piled up, or their constant, ever-changing needs.

And even when the days were long for her, she continued to surprise me. Our sex life was as rich as ever. We were both as attracted to each other as we'd been from the day I showed up outside the news station. In fact, I was more attracted to her now than that day, something I never thought would have been possible.

I loved knowing that things would never grow stale in our relationship.

After flashing me a brilliant smile, Sage asked, "Is everything ready to go? Do you have all the boards?"

Shaking my head with a grin on my face, I said, "I'm going to give you the same response I gave our daughter when she asked me her own version of that very question only a few minutes ago. When have I ever not had the boards ready?"

Sage rolled her eyes at me but made no response.

I did.

"I haven't seen Hunter since he left the breakfast table this morning," I started. "I assume he's ready to go."

Cocking an eyebrow at me, Sage returned, "When have I ever not had our babies ready to go?"

"Fair enough. What about you?"

"Me?" she asked.

I nodded. "Yeah. Are you ready to go?"

"We're heading out for a fun-filled day as a family, Gunner," Sage began. "Try and stop me."

My eyes searched her face. It would have been easy to stare at her all day long.

Apparently, I must have done that for too long because she called, "Gunner?"

Blinking my eyes and returning back to the present moment, I replied, "Yeah?"

"What's going through your mind?" she asked. "I can tell you're thinking about something."

I shook my head before I assured her, "It's nothing."

"It's not nothing."

Following a brief pause, I admitted, "It's just that sometimes I can't believe I'm here."

"What do you mean?"

"With you," I started. "All these years have passed and I still find myself in such disbelief that you and I are here together. If that wasn't enough of a reward for me, you've given me Ivy and Hunter."

Sage leaned her weight into me. "I couldn't have given you those babies on my own," she noted.

Nodding, I claimed, "I know that. But I feel so lucky to be here with you and with them. I never realized how much I needed the three of you until I had all of you."

My wife tipped her head back, pressed up on her

toes, and kissed me. "I think the kids and I are the lucky ones."

"We'll have to agree to disagree on this one," I said softly.

"Can we go now?" Hunter called out, interrupting our moment.

Sage and I turned our attention to our son.

"Yes, baby, we're coming now," Sage answered him. "Let's head out to the car."

Ivy had entered the room moments after Hunter, but at Sage's words, they both turned and raced off toward the garage.

Sage looked back at me and said, "We better get going."

"Go ahead out with them," I urged her. "I'll grab the bag and be right out."

Sage gave me another kiss before following behind our children. I watched her as she walked away.

Then I bent down and picked up our gear bag, feeling grateful that this was now my responsibility.

My wife. My children. Taking care of them brought me more happiness than I could have ever hoped for.

While it might have seemed like a lot of work, it didn't bother me. Because when I thought back to how low I had been feeling all those years ago, I knew how lucky I was. My family had revived me and given me the chance to live out my dream.

Seeing them happy was all that mattered to me.

Watching my children pursue their dreams, knowing I was able to give that to them, meant everything.

And that was precisely what happened two weeks later when Ivy and Hunter both won their respective classes at the Blackman Boards contest.

When they walked up to the podium and received their

trophies, I never could have imagined that it would make me feel better than I did when I'd won a snowboarding contest myself all those years ago.

But it did.

And it was all thanks to the woman who'd ran into my arms outside a news station nearly nine years ago.

ACKNOWLEDGEMENTS

To my husband, Jeff—My love. Thank you for being my sounding board. Your support means everything to me. I love you.

To my boys, J&J—My little loves… I can't get over how much you've grown since I started this series. Thank you for giving me so much of my kid material. I love you so much.

To my loyal readers—Thank you for falling in love with my Cunningham Security team. I'm so grateful for your growing enthusiasm with each story in this series.

To S.H., S.B., & E.M.—Covers, formatting, and editing. I've got the best team. Thanks to each of you for all of your hard work on making this series everything that it is.

To the bloggers—Thank you, thank you, thank you!!

CONNECT WITH A.K. EVANS

To stay connected with A.K. Evans and receive all the first looks at upcoming releases, latest news, or to simply follow along on her journey, be sure to add or follow her on social media. You can also get the scoop by signing up for the monthly newsletter, which includes a giveaway every month.

Newsletter: http://eepurl.com/dmeo6z

Website: www.authorakevans.com

Facebook: www.facebook.com/authorAKEvans

Facebook Reader Group: www.facebook.com/groups/1285069088272037

Instagram: www.instagram.com/authorakevans

Twitter: twitter.com/AuthorAKEvans

Goodreads Author Page: www.goodreads.com/user/show/64525877-a-k-evans

Subscribe on YouTube: http://bit.ly2w01yb7

Twitter: twitter.com/AuthorAKEvans

OTHER BOOKS BY A.K. EVANS

The Everything Series
Everything I Need
Everything I Have
Everything I Want
Everything I Love

The Cunningham Security Series

Obsessed
Overcome
Desperate
Solitude
Burned
Unworthy
Surrender
Betrayed
Revived

Road Trip Romance

Tip the Scales
Play the Part
One Wrong Turn
Just a Fling
Meant to Be
Take the Plunge (Coming July 14, 2020)
Miss the Shot (Coming Fall 2020)

ABOUT A.K. EVANS

A.K. Evans is a married mother of two boys residing in a small town in northeastern Pennsylvania, where she graduated from Lafayette College in 2004 with two degrees (one in English and one in Economics & Business). Following a brief stint in the insurance and financial services industry, Evans realized the career was not for her and went on to manage her husband's performance automotive business. She even drove the shop's race cars! Looking for more personal fulfillment after eleven years in the automotive industry, Andrea decided to pursue her dream of becoming a writer.

While Andrea continues to help administratively with her husband's businesses, she spends most of her time writing and homeschooling her two boys. When she finds scraps of spare time, Evans enjoys reading, doing yoga, watching NY Rangers hockey, dancing, and vacationing with her family. Andrea, her husband, and her children are currently working on taking road trips to visit all 50 states (though, Alaska and Hawaii might require flights).

Made in the USA
Columbia, SC
12 June 2022